BELOVED SA MI

A River Han: Book One

J.M. Hong

To My Beloveds: Mina and Max

RO7101 81067

*And in the beginning there were the heavens above,
and the earth below,
a black hole of yellow swirling dust.
The cosmos were wide and rough...*

-*Chunja Moon*

PART I: MARRIAGE

Two strangers
joined by Fate,
destiny-bound
and entangled
in vines of memory,
Sow gilded stories
from blood-tears
like blooms of petals
embedded in our veins.

Beloved *Mangnae*

September 1916

Gwangju, Chollanam-do Province, Korea

The new Japanese Governor General of Chosen (Korea) had assumed his post less than nine days when Sa Mi walked out to the outhouse to relieve herself, only to make an unsettling discovery.

Her lady-in-waiting, also known as Jumjaengy, (a double reference to the cherry-colored birthmark that covered her left eye and her gift of prophecy), reacted quickly and threw open the door just in time to catch her swooning master. Sa Mi's skirt was still bunched under her arms and her underpants were around her ankles with a fresh crimson stain down the middle when Jumjaengy reached out to her.

It was shock and callous reality that seized Sa Mi in that moment. With three older sisters Sa Mi was not naïve to the ways of the world. She knew that she was not bleeding to death or that she had sustained some sort of life-threatening ailment or injury for that matter.

The source of Sa Mi's disappointment was that this cruel and unwelcome event made her a woman when she was nowhere near ready for the constraints of that role. Sa Mi was far more comfortable being her parents' *mangnae*, or the doted-on youngest child, in that hallowed house of ghosts and shadows.

After Sa Mi came to her senses and cleaned herself up with the help of Jumjaengy who insisted she lie down with a cup of tea, Sa Mi made her swear that the secret remain between the two of them.

"You must promise not to share this with *anyone*," Sa Mi said, lowering her swollen eyes at her servant.

"Of course *agassi*. Who else might I tell except your mother?"

"*Especially* my mother," Sa Mi hissed, hearing her mother's voice in the courtyard, then repeating for emphasis, "No one!"

"But *agassi*, please, you cannot expect me to keep something like this from your mo…" But before she could finish the matron of the house entered the room and Jumjaengy was up on her feet bowing her head at Sa Mi's mother.

"What is going on here?" the dignified woman inquired, then seeing the pale face of her youngest daughter, her beloved *mangnae* resting on the pillow, "My goodness!" she gasped, hurrying to Sa Mi's side in concern.

"I'm sorry," the humbled servant replied, bearing responsibility for the ill fate of her master. "*Agassi* may have overexerted herself this morning in the garden. It seems we still have not shaken off this long winter. The spring air is still nippy."

Sa Mi looked hopefully at her mother, grateful that Jumjaengy had not betrayed her.

"Didn't I tell you not to stay too long outside?" Sa Mi's mother started gently, stroking the stray hair from her daughter's face. "It is still cold…and it is not becoming of a young lady to be running around like that. You are not still a child," she said, though her coddling ways toward Sa Mi belied her own words.

"But *omonee*, I am fine. *Ajumma* has made me some tea and I am resting now. Besides, father does not mind me out in the garden. We have been reviewing the different plants and their characteristics."

Sa Mi's mother let out a sigh. It was evident to everyone that they had not raised their youngest in the proper *yangban* form by allowing her a freedom that appeared far too indulgent in the eyes of others. Minjung had felt like a failure after being unable to produce an heir for her husband after giving birth to four daughters. This disappointment was all her own however, because Sa Mi's father never hinted at being bereft of a son, and instead, lauded the extraordinary efforts and successes of his youngest daughter.

Indeed, Minjung blamed her husband for spoiling Sa Mi. While Minjung was trying to smooth things over with the other mothers who expressed their concerns that Sa Mi was challenging their sons again at one feat or another, Sa Mi's father would later stroll into the house, chuckling about how much smarter, faster, and more competent Sa Mi was than any of the neighborhood *yangban* boys.

The constant messaging Sa Mi received as a young girl was that there was no need for a son. And for her to be so rudely shaken into her true station in life seemed like a cruel fate. Like her sisters, and the societal expectations that had been laid out for her for generations, she too would eventually marry into another family and become part of that world of strangers. Unlike her male counterparts, marriage was the best that she could hope for in life. And despite her father's amusement, it didn't much matter whether she was better at anything than the neighborhood boys. The stain on her underwear only propelled her further toward the inevitable.

For the moment, Sa Mi wanted to wallow in her suffering, and felt there was no immediate need for her parents to share in the lousy news of her recent ascent into womanhood. Besides, her father was far too busy to be bothered by such trifles. Ever since the new governor general arrived her father left home early and returned late in the evening.

Sa Mi's father represented their district in the local government, which suited him well. As one of the most prominent landlords in the district, Son Chaesu was well-respected for his moral rectitude and expansive intellect which allowed him to analyze and sort through problems with care and an eye for detail. Sa Mi's father was of the uncommon breed. His impeccable posture and dignified presence aligned with his open character. In his public affairs Chaesu stood-up boldly for the way of justice and continued to do so when such acts were considered naïve and politically suicidal; all while his colleagues scrambled to ally with factions that would ensure their power during the chaos that prefaced the Japanese takeover.

In his steady and deep voice, warm, but unwavering, he would declare to his enthusiastic supporters, "Like the reeds of the riverbed we may bend to the winds of change, but we will never break. Our history remains firmly rooted in this stubborn earth and the steadfast river that runs through it." Chaesu knew the urgency and earnestness of his message carried with it a tremendous risk.

The ongoing problem of the Japanese occupation was one with no easy answers that plagued Sa Mi's father day and night, aging him prematurely and causing him to hold firm to his humanitarian principles whatever the price. The rumors preceding the new governor general's arrival had not been promising and if Chaesu's strained demeanor every evening was any indication of what the country could hope for under the new leadership – which was rumored to be hard line, militaristic, and with a policy of eradicating the Korean culture – Chaesu had a hard fight before him. He often said that the spirit of his supporters held him up, but Sa Mi could tell that on some days, the Japanese could crack the stoicism so painstakingly etched onto her father's face.

After half-heartedly scolding Sa Mi for pushing the expectation of proper decorum, Minjung gave a skeptical eye toward the humbled servant and left the room. There were others already making preparations in the kitchen for the family dinner that evening at their home. Sa Mi's older sisters and their families were all coming over to discuss the recent developments in the nationalist movement and the Japanese imperial policy under the new leadership.

#

First and foremost, a man must have his freedom. It is freedom after all that gives birth to ideas and innovation. It is freedom that restores civility and allows mankind to advance and progress in his lonely station toward a common and communal good.

The father of four had mulled these words over in his mind, time and again.

"Freedom is the most basic tenet in a human life," Chaesu proposed, "and to impinge on a man's freedom throughout the course of his daily life is to erode at the very thing that makes him human."

Chaesu was no radical, but he couldn't remain silent about the complicity he witnessed among his countrymen in holding up the colonial regime. He was a progressive thinker, and while the occupation had come with some modern improvements in the country's infrastructure and propelled the hermit kingdom into a new age, Chaesu was unconvinced that the Japanese ought to be credited for what he perceived as an inevitable turning of events, nor could he accept that such modern advances come at the price of individual freedom.

"It is a price we must all pay," his friend posited, "to get us out of the dark ages."

"Perhaps there is an element of that. That we must make sacrifices toward progress. But it is precisely during times of change that we must be vigilant. After all, it is only from independent thought that innovative ideas can be birthed. What we need during these trying times is humanity at its best. We have a responsibility, especially those of us that have some means."

"The daily demands are great my friend, and sometimes it is all we can do to take care of our families."

"Of course. We must care for our families, for our futures. This is precisely why we cannot bury our heads in the sand. We are all in this together. We cannot turn our backs on our fellow countrymen," Chaesu pleaded with his friend.

"One thing about you is that you never give up," Taejun declared with a surrendering tone. "At what point do you feel blinded by your own idealism?"

"It is not so much idealism my friend than a hunger for a basic human right. A right that every man ought to be entitled. If we give up, what hope do we have as a society? As a nation?"

Taejun eyed him nervously, "You speak of hope my friend, and I wonder if you are not thinking about it the wrong way. Perhaps our best hope is to make the most out of what is a hopeless situation," then, "Are you not going to drink your *sul*? It is getting cold. My wife had it fermenting all winter. It is good for your senses, your spirits. Please..." gesturing with his hand for Chaesu to take a sip.

Chaesu glanced down at the cup, and then looked up at his friend. "I've never heard such fatalistic words in my life. If that makes me an idealist, thank God for that. Are you listening to what I'm saying? We are not Japanese. We must continue to resist this occupation, no matter the price." Chaesu then raised his cup and emptied it into his throat, feeling it burn down his insides.

The color drained from Taejun's face for a split second, not long enough for Chaesu to notice, but just enough to cast a shadow over Taejun's expression, allowing him to acknowledge what he had just done.

Quickly he recovered, "Yes. I understand. We live in such harrowing times," then quoting from Chaesu's previous speech, "We must elect the path of the righteous; we must ensure the future of our children, of the earth below them, of the history that precedes them..." Taejun's voice strained as he lowered his head and looked into the eyes of his childhood friend, "You know, you always stood out Chaesu-ya. You were always the smartest, the most courageous, the one everyone listens to, the one everyone loves...I know this has been hard on you my friend."

Chaesu let out a sigh, "Indeed it has taken a toll on us all. And without friends like you to hold me up, I am nothing. Alone we suffer our blows most palpably in silence. But together, together we are a force. So...what do you say?"

"Yes," Taejun whispered, the weight of his action seizing him. "We are nothing if we are alone. You have my word Chaesu-ya. My loyalties are with you. I must still send Kitae to school in Japan, I hope you can understand. But I cannot be bought by these people. I won't be bought. Our roots in this land are too deep my friend," with this Taejun turned his head as tears welled up in eyes.

10

Chaesu stood up, moved by his friend's transformation. "You won't regret this. I'll do everything in my power to ensure your safety. If we are guided by our principles, we cannot, will not, be corrupted," Then rubbing his chest, "I must go now. Today my daughters are gathering at my house. Who knows what chaos awaits me?"

"Yes, yes of course," Taejun recovered, standing and taking note of Chaesu's discomfort as he rubbed his chest. "It is a beautiful evening though. It would be a shame not to enjoy a leisurely walk home."

"Yes. Thank you. A nice walk will do me some good. Until next time," and with a smile Chaesu departed.

Taejun stood and watched the silhouette of his friend walk away from him until he could see him no longer. He wondered if his suggestion for a long walk might spare the family that adored Chaesu from watching him suffer in his final moments.

Chaesu paused from his steady pace to catch his breath again. Something was not right. His chest felt tight and his head was throbbing when he looked up to see a Shinto shrine up ahead.

Earlier in the evening he had wanted to belt out at Taejun, "Where's your spirit? Do you not see what is happening around you?" But instead he pointed at his graying hair and the creases on his face and stated, "This is not in vain. To all who have suffered so much, this is nothing." Taejun's son was soon leaving to study in Kyoto. And while Chaesu endured the same humiliation of all the landowners who had visits from Japanese officers to monitor their activities and rice yields, Taejun had been shown some mercy from the Japanese. The mercy had the effect of blotting out the greater injustices of his fellow countrymen, and it was clear that Chaesu's friend was not exerting any energies to oppose the regime that offered his family a way in the changing world.

11

For Taejun to change his mind so dramatically in the conversation was unexpected. Chaesu was pleased to hear it, but the rate at which the alcohol shot through his body distracted him. He tried to focus but was overwhelmed by confusion and dizziness.

Chaesu looked up at the stars that appeared to race across the sky. His chest was growing tighter. He grabbed his throat as he felt his airways closing in. It had all happened so fast. How many times had he accepted a drink from his friend? Was Taejun truly capable of such a thing? As his body shut down Chaesu saw the image of his friend staring him in his eyes during that moment of atonement. He had done it. Nobody would know.

As death gripped him and his body began to convulse, people ran up to the charming landlord who was their local hero as he struggled to fend off the effect of the poison. But it was too late. With his last breath he recalled images of his beloved family, and the one person whose spirit ran toward him was his treasured *mangnae*, Sa Mi. Then, his heart stopped.

Later, they would refer to it as a cardiac arrest, brought on by the stresses of the Japanese occupation.

Chaesu hit the pavement and all went black.

#

Gatherings with her daughters were rare now that they were grown and busy with their own families and observing their obligations as wives and daughters-in-law. It had been some time since Minjung had shared a meal with all of her daughters and she was looking forward to seeing how each was faring in their lives and no less eager to see her grandchildren. A force in the kitchen,

Minjung was not one to let anything past her without her express blessings. As the noise in the kitchen drew nearer, Minjung rolled up her sleeves to put her stamp on the delicious smells that emanated from the kitchen.

"Agassi...agassi!" Jumjaengy whispered, gently tapping on her master's shoulders to prod her awake.

Sa Mi groaned, and then blinked before sitting up. As she ran her hands through her hair, Jumjaengy used her master's porcelain comb to section Sa Mi's hair into her signature two braids.

Not saying a word Sa Mi let out a sigh as Jumjaengy parted her hair. As her senses returned to her, Sa Mi realized she would have to accept the fact that she was now a young woman and prepare herself before facing the rest of her family.

"Are they all here?" Sa Mi inquired reluctantly, wishing to stay in her bed.

"Your sisters are all helping your mother in the kitchen. The men are in the courtyard smoking and talking. The children are scattered throughout, and your father has not yet arrived."

"You didn't say anything to them, did you?" Sa Mi confirmed, her eyes expectant.

"No. But you must. Your mother will leave me out in the cold when she discovers my deception. Besides, it is a joyful occasion. Your ladyship should be pleased," she added cheerfully.

Sa Mi stayed quiet in anticipation of seeing her sisters in her current state. Would they be able to tell? Would her mother be able to tell? Was there a universal and cosmic force among women that allowed them to discern such things? Even worse, would her

13

brothers-in-law be able to tell? Her father?! The thought made Sa Mi want to bury her head into the security of her blankets. She was filled with shame. Shame for having been born a girl.

After *ajumma* finished braiding Sa Mi's hair, Sa Mi dressed in her finest *hanbok* which had been cleaned and pressed for the occasion, then took a deep breath and made her way toward the kitchen and the sounds of the other women in her family.

Despite the prying eyes of the Japanese monitoring the rice yield of his estate, Sa Mi's father was still able to maintain enough rice for his family's consumption. For large gatherings like this however, Sa Mi's mother often mixed barley into the rice to stretch it further and worked her infinite magic on the mushroom shoots and greens that sprouted from the earth this time of year to simmer soups and other side dishes.

Sa Mi's sisters had all learned the art of cooking from their mother and were forces in the kitchen in their own right. When they all came together one knew that an unparalleled feast was forthcoming. Sa Mi was the only one who didn't contribute to the meals. Her mother thought the labors of the kitchen too lowly for her intellectual youngest daughter and often shooed her away from such chores. Instead, Sa Mi wove back and forth from the gossip of her sisters to the lively antics of her nieces and nephews who adored on her. Sa Mi realized this evening would be no different as soon as she set foot in the kitchen.

"Well, look who it is," Ock, Sa Mi's second oldest sister and the most outspoken of the bunch started, "the princess has decided to arrive!" her mouth turned up wryly in the corner.

"Sa Mi-ya!" Heebin called out with a smile walking toward her and laying the back of her hand gently to her sister's forehead, "Are you feeling okay? You do look pale you poor thing." Though Heebin was closest in age to her, she was the most caring and showed the most affection toward Sa Mi.

"Still?!" their mother cried out, her hands covered in red pepper paste.

"*Ahnyung eonni*," Sa Mi greeted all three of her older sisters with a smile. "I am fine, just waking up from my nap." Young, Sa Mi's oldest sister and of the fewest words, simply nodded in Sa Mi's direction and carried on with her frying duties for the *pajun*, a savory pancake filled with delights such as the shrimp that had just been caught in the morning.

"Sa Mi, now that you are well rested, come over here and help me cut this *kimchi*," Ock cried out playfully, with an expectant ear toward her mother.

"Ai yah! No. Leave her alone. Sa Mi, you can watch us, no need to muddy up your fingers. Besides, she is still too young to be using the knives…"

But before her mother could finish Sa Mi had rolled up her sleeves and joined her sisters who were all exchanging glances with one another.

"Mother! Too young indeed. I don't recall any of us being spared kitchen duty when we were Sa Mi's age," Ock started.

"That's not true," chimed in Young, "Heebin had to preserve her fingers for playing. I think you and I had the brunt of the kitchen work."

"A lot of good preserving my fingers does for me now," Heebin said quietly as their mother, too shocked to respond to her daughters' insolence quickly wiped her hands with a dish towel and lunged for her youngest before Sa Mi's hands plunged into a vat of salted cabbage.

"Sa Mi, don't listen to them. Stand and watch if you like, go see your nieces and nephews, but please don't make a mess of your *hanbok*. As for you ungrateful girls, I will remind you that Sa

Mi is unwell today, and that you two always enjoyed working with me in the kitchen. Heebin couldn't ruin her hands for the piano any more than Sa Mi should blemish her hands to poise a pen. We all have our talents," declared Minjung with an air of self-righteousness.

"If I become any more talented at housework you will have to give me a trophy," sighed Ock.

"How about satiating your mother-in-law?" groaned Young to which Heebin quickly replied, "I shall take myself out of the running, I shall never come close to achieving that!" she quipped.

Sa Mi's mother clucked her tongue in rebuke though it was clear that she was enjoying her daughters' company.

"In all seriousness mother, do you really think you are doing Sa Mi any favors when her fate is to end up like ours, married and at the mercy of our in-laws?"

Sa Mi hated it when her sisters talked about her as if she wasn't there and countered, "Who says I am to be married? I am only fifteen."

Ignoring her sister Ock continued, "Look at Heebin. Forgive me for speaking out of turn, but how has her piano playing helped her in her daily existence?" glancing an eye to her sister.

The proud mother had had enough, "I beg your pardon? Heebin is able to make her own money from her piano lessons."

"Yes," started Heebin, "and because I teach to the neighborhood Japanese children, mother-in-law insists that I am a Japanese collaborator because of it."

"She actually said that to you?!" Ock asked in disbelief as the others groaned.

Heebin nodded. "And anyway, Ock is right. It is a double-edged sword. Mother-in-law looks down on it, but I wouldn't know what to do without my piano in that oppressive house, it keeps me sane. But it certainly doesn't help me get the meals served on time," then pausing and turning her head to Sa Mi, "In that regard you ought to keep studying no matter what your situation. Otherwise you will end up like them," she whispered pointing at their sisters, "with nothing to keep you sane!"

This made Sa Mi smile as Ock responded by chucking a bean sprout Heebin's way.

"Listen to all of you complain. We should be counting our blessings during these uncertain times. You have all married into respectable families and when the time is right so will Sa Mi," the matriarch offered, putting an end to the conversation.

"The way all of you go on and on about your married lives, marriage is further away from my thoughts than you can imagine," Sa Mi added.

"See what you've done?" Minjung leveled, raising her eyebrows at her daughters, who appeared to be more like girlfriends than children for whom she was once responsible.

To rescue them all from this line of questioning in ran Ock's oldest son and Heebin's two girls. As soon as they saw Sa Mi they screeched "*E-mo!*" for their favorite aunt, tugging and pulling on her to join the rest of the children. Ock's two younger children, a boy and a girl, were with Young's son and daughter who were close in age to Sa Mi. Given Sa Mi's age they thought of her more as a cousin than they did an aunt.

"*E-mo, e-mo* come play!" little Jungwha squealed with delight. Sa Mi looked up at her mother.

"Go, go, go play!" Sa Mi's mother replied. "Why don't you children go pick some flowers from the garden?" she suggested.

17

Sa Mi smiled as she hopped up and ran alongside her nieces and nephew. No one had suspected a thing. There was still plenty of child in her despite Mother Nature's interruption. There was still so much freedom to be had.

The One Certainty

Love is all that is certain and nothing else, her mother had whispered to Sa Mi on the final day of the mourning ceremony for her father. *Love is all that is certain*, Sa Mi repeated desperately to herself over and over again as she now stared at the pale and lifeless corpse of her mother.

Love is all that is certain, Sa Mi said, trying to seek solace in the same words that passed through her mother's lips. But it was in vain. For it was more than the abstraction of love that she craved, it was her parents' physical presence that she longed for. It was the soft fold in her mother's arm, the sweet smell of camellia that emanated from her hair, the sharp angle of her father's jaw, his scholarly gaze, and his warm, velvet voice that she wanted so desperately to hear, see, and smell.

The sudden death of her father had clipped Sa Mi's youthful wings. Buoyed by the sheer force of maternal love, Sa Mi endured by holding fast to her mother, but when the autumn wind whisked her mother's soul away, Sa Mi found herself on a swift and certain downward spiral. The permanence of her parents' deaths had robbed Sa Mi from her life as she knew it. In the desperation of the moments that followed, the solace of her parents' love was a comfort she found to be utterly useless. She was too overcome with sorrow. The shock paralyzed her.

The day had started out like any other since her father died. As they approached the one-year mark Minjung's despondency began to lift. And though she refused to venture outside the estate, she faithfully packed Sa Mi's lunch for school every day, served her daughter breakfast, and saw her out the door. It was just the two of them now, and Minjung knew she had to find it in herself to be strong though she had no idea of how she was to live, or how to keep moving forward in their lives without her steadfast husband.

After Sa Mi left for school Minjung passed by the garden that was her husband's laboratory for teaching his captive youngest daughter about the plodding and diligent labors of cultivating life, and about how Nature prevailed in even the most unlikely circumstances. Neither Minjung nor Sa Mi had tended it since Chaesu's death and despite their neglect, the perennials still burst from the soil and the garden was still fodder for the deer that came around this time of year. Minjung pondered the garden before her when she spotted some weeds. For the first time in almost a year she bent down to pull them when she felt a squeeze on her heart that brought her gracefully to her knees on that October morning. After whispering the name of her angel, her treasure Sa Mi, she clutched onto her chest as her large breasts fell into the soft dusty earth below.

Meanwhile, at the sight of her principal's somber face whispering in her teacher's ear, Sa Mi ran out the school door and sprinted all the way home to where her mother had collapsed just as naturally as a flower wilting in the rain, and not the thunderclap one would expect from such a strong, uncompromising woman. Sa Mi knelt down in anguish, tears streaming down her face as her calls of *omonee* echoed over the mountaintop.

But it was too late.

The soul of her mother had already spread to the distant stars, carried by the fierce autumn wind.

And so, Sa Mi found herself chanting the same words that came from her mother after her father's death not one-year earlier. *Love is all that is certain*, she heard herself say. *Love is all that is certain*, she repeated over and over again to herself as she peered at her mother's corpse. *Love is all that is certain*, was the mantra she clung to like a life preserver. *Love is all that is certain*, she said; certain, that she too was part dead herself.

Soon after the formal mourning period for her mother, a bitter tension seized the surviving family members as Sa Mi's sisters and their husbands disputed over her parents' estate. The tragedy of not having a male heir did not escape Sa Mi's father, but unlike his contemporaries he often took pride in telling people he had four beautiful daughters though they often returned his declaration with a look of pity and an extension of their condolences. Without a male heir, the seizure of the family's land and property by the colonial government was a foregone conclusion. That Chaesu's tender heart was halted by his childhood friend was just one of the cruel realities of living under the occupation.

As their beloved *mangnae*, Sa Mi had spent many of her years as an only child alone with her parents, her sisters having long been married and out of the house. In that village of theirs, where news travels faster than the wind, everyone would whisper about how the older couple would ever manage without their youngest daughter who hurried home every day after school to see them. People gossiped that the couple secretly hoped to grow old with their *mangnae*, cheating her out of marriage and a future with her own family (as if the selfish joys of parenthood ever outweighs the persistent worry of what lies ahead). Those nosy neighbors surmised that the unbreakable bond the couple shared

21

with their youngest was the reason why they did not appear to be in any hurry to find her a suitable mate like they had done with their other three daughters.

Even when Sa Mi's mother was prematurely swept into the shadows of widowhood, people were assuaged by the fact that she still had her beloved *mangnae* whose existence fueled her own desire to live each day and set foot upon the rocky earth. No one doubted that she would be able to achieve the arduous feat of raising and educating her youngest child given the combination of her blind determination, sturdy constitution, and that timeless and enduring anodyne of maternal love.

That Fate could so abruptly intervene in Minjung's endeavor was just another sign of the times when uncertainty plagued the soil of that forlorn nation. After her mother followed Sa Mi's father to the dark unknown, Sa Mi sought desperately to find her way among her crippling despair. She could not understand how her sisters could talk, much less argue about the mundane details left behind from their mother's death. They talked all around death but never confronted it while Sa Mi asphyxiated in its aftermath.

Before she knew what had happened, Sa Mi was hurried away to the home of her eldest sister. Though this sister and her husband ended up with most of what remained of her parents' estate, Young was disappointed to learn that she would have to take in Sa Mi as well.

Sa Mi had always been apprehensive about the little she knew about this sister who was sixteen years her senior. Young was married and out of the house while Sa Mi was still in diapers, and despite the close proximity of her home, rarely visited her parents and other siblings. Always observing the height of formality, Young was aloof in her interactions and one could not differentiate her tone when she was addressing her family or entertaining the important guests her husband would often bring home. Her restrained personality – Sa Mi's parents felt – was exacerbated by the fact that she had married early into a home of high officials who on more than one occasion looked down on Sa Mi's family. When it became evident that the young couple's political loyalties were as fickle as a chameleon's cloak – for they shamelessly yielded to power and recognition – Young and her husband grew ever more distant from Sa Mi's parents who often slowly shook their heads or sighed with regret at the mention of this sister.

"She must remain a loyal and faithful daughter-in-law and wife to her family," Sa Mi's father would start, his tone clearly indicating his longing for his eldest daughter. "May the gods watch over her and bring her family fortune and prosperity."

Sa Mi sat quietly during those moments though she could not help but feel a sting of betrayal at seeing her father's hurt eyes. She saw how marriage could divide you from your natal family. Sa Mi could never imagine being separated from her parents.

No matter where life leads me I shall always be there as a comfort for my parents. No man and his family will have such influence over me, Sa Mi had asserted in the self-righteous security of her parents' care.

And yet, in the confusion of those days after the spirits had laid claim on her mother, Sa Mi was swept into the hushed formality of her eldest sister's home where Young and her husband dwelled with her mother-in-law and four children, the oldest of whom was not but a few years younger than Sa Mi.

Sa Mi was unaffected when the stern-faced mother-in-law acknowledged her only with a cold nod, or when her brother-in-law did not acknowledge her at all, or when the children looked at her with a guarded curiosity, but when her sister treated her as if she were a stranger (and perhaps, as a lingering nuisance) and addressed her only when it was absolutely necessary, Sa Mi felt her sorrows joined by a sickening loneliness which fueled a paralyzing and torrential fever.

As she lied quarantined in a room cared for by servants and the occasional visit from her sister scolding her to get better, she caught bits of conversations between her sister and the mother-in-law about plans for marrying Sa Mi into a family referred to them by a matchmaker, whose in-laws would not object to the meager dowry that *they* had to offer. Sa Mi perked her ears to make sure that this was not another fever-induced delusion and when dawn ascended, a confused and startled servant woke the lady of the house to show her that the shadow of a girl with a fever was no longer there.

Walking Alone

The heavy lid of a crescent moon veiled the night with darkness when Sa Mi quietly closed the gate of her oldest sister's house forever. She looked up to see that the curve of the moon matched the white jade pendant that hung around her neck like a tear drop, signifying her mother's permanent exit from the world and Sa Mi's broken state. As she looked up at the night sky, she pressed her lips against the cold, smooth surface of the pendant that once graced the neck of her own mother, then placed her long braid around her shoulder and lifted the corner of her *hanbok*, before stepping into the cold uncertainty of night.

Her biggest fear at this time of night were the Japanese policemen who swarm the streets like beetles, ready to quell any uprisings and agitation from the rebel Koreans. Though it was mid-August there was an eerie chill in the air that made Sa Mi shiver. She had not yet recovered from her fever, which, combined with the cool, wet darkness had a hallucinating effect on her and only seemed to magnify her fear.

Squinting at the darkness, Sa Mi took one step after another toward the home of her next oldest sister, Ock, with nothing but a change of clothes wrapped up in her *podegi* which she clutched in her right hand. As Sa Mi walked she sought to quell the sound of her breath which she was sure would invite the police her way. She had already decided that she would never return to her sister Young's house with whom she shared nothing but blood and a history that was no longer relevant, and if caught, she would lie and say she had come from a friend's home. For now, she struggled to take deep, steady breaths to calm the ringing in her ears and rhythmically wiped the sweat off her brow with the arm of her *hanbok*.

Sa Mi did not want to find out first-hand what the Japanese did to young girls roaming the streets alone at that hour. When they were alive her parents expressly forbid her to go anywhere unescorted. Though they adhered to the convention of the times that no proper girl ought to be roaming the streets without an escort, they also sought to terrify Sa Mi with stories of young Korean girls who had been kidnapped and sent to work on labor camps for the Japanese. In the event that Society's judgment was not enough to deter Sa Mi from roaming the streets alone for fear of being branded a certain type of girl, Sa Mi's mother drove the point home by flooding her *mangnae's* mind with images of young Korean girls whose faulty judgment of disobeying their parents' orders had led them to become victim to Japanese cruelty.

Sa Mi sought to bury those images in the back of her mind as she picked up her pace and found the *swish swish* from the silk skirt of her *hanbok*, the irrepressible pant of her breath, and the pounding of her feet onto the dense earth as certain to invite suspicion. Without allowing herself to contemplate the possible outcomes to her plight, Sa Mi focused on the fact that she had nothing more to lose. Life had taken away the anchors to her existence, her only hope in a society that condemned the lonely child, the orphan, the ones that are left behind. Overnight, Sa Mi had become like one of them.

It was a blind optimism that she had cultivated under the safe haven of her parents' watch. Despite her parents' political leanings, Sa Mi learned to win the favor of her Japanese teachers by priding herself on the mastery of the language and observing a compliant resignation and not the bitter sorrow of the oppressed.

She believed that the indignities she suffered under the Japanese were nothing more than harsh truths, the inevitable outcome of grown-ups and their games that resulted in torment for some and an exultation of others. She didn't take the abuses as a personal assault. As there were always sides to be taken in such conflicts, Sa Mi surmised, so was there destined to be suffering.

Sa Mi's parents had gone to great lengths to protect their youngest from the imprint of the occupation, but despite their best efforts the brutality hung in the air like feasting vultures, raw and insatiable. Sa Mi shifted her gaze from the more obvious savages of the occupation and aimed to forgive what she perceived as dramas controlled by far greater forces. In her deferential manner, Sa Mi sought to preserve the peace of her personal life against a backdrop of upheaval and chaos. In some ways, she felt, the rebellion itself was responsible for her father's death. Martyrs only seemed to serve abstract causes and uncertain outcomes, it was the predictability of everyday and the assured steps of the routine and familiar that mattered to Sa Mi.

The way to her second oldest sister's house was quiet and desolate this time of night. Ock lived about three miles down the main dirt road which was dotted with residences and open fields bursting with wild rose-colored cosmos and Korean pine. The elusive jagged peaks of mountains that offset the village to the West looked ominous in the velvet sky, and the sheer expanse of the geography made Sa Mi feel as if the earth might crack open and swallow her whole. Up ahead, Sa Mi saw the lights from a small tavern burning in a subversive glow as drunken laughter pierced forth into the night. Sa Mi sought to distance herself from it by walking swiftly on the opposite edge of the road.

When she found that she had safely cleared the vicinity of the tavern without anyone noticing, she let out a sigh of relief. She was three-quarters of the way to Ock's house and though her palms were slick with sweat and her thoughts diffuse from her lingering fever, Sa Mi felt a sudden exhilaration for nearly completing a feat she never thought possible. For the first time since her parents' death, she experienced the freedom that often accompanies the shadow of loneliness, it was a sense of empowerment that took her by surprise. But all of a sudden, Sa Mi gasped and felt the pulse of her heart halt at the sound of a man's voice.

"*Agassi!*" he whispered sharply at her, "*Agassi,* stop!" his voice hissed from behind her.

Her legs leaden with fear, Sa Mi kept her head down and walked as quickly as her heavy feet would carry her, somehow too crippled with dread to break out into a full sprint.

Before long she felt him grab her by her shoulder and when she instinctively pulled herself away and opened her mouth to scream, he tightly covered the bottom half of her face with a rough hand that reeked of tobacco and dragged her behind a nearby ginkgo tree.

He pushed her back up against the trunk so she could see the alcohol-hungry gleam in his eye and a scar that ran down the left side of the shadowy stubble of his cheek.

In that moment of panic, Sa Mi thought that she was about to experience that unnamable tragedy that befalls young women like her, leaving them ruined forever. A girl like her was perpetually standing at the precipice of certain ruin. It was that cursed coincidence of birth which made girls female that the men in their lives sought to both protect and violate. Her fragile existence hinged on this dichotomy of virtue and shame; blind luck, it seemed, was what dictated on which side a young girl would end up.

So this was what people talked about when they clicked their tongues or narrowed their eyebrows, wondered Sa Mi. Growing up in the shelter of her parents' watch, Sa Mi never quite knew exactly what the tragedy was, she only feared in that moment that she was about to experience it in the hands of the vagabond before her. Longing, fear, loss; this was what characterized the rhythm of Sa Mi's life as of late.

"I'm not going to hurt you *agassi*," he hissed in her ear, the cigarette-laden heat of his breath causing her to cower.

"Just give me your money and I'll be on my way," he demanded firmly.

"*Your money!*" he repeated gruffly as he grabbed both of her arms, nervously looking over his own shoulders.

After seeing Sa Mi's dumbfounded face, he began searching her skirt for a purse, before she cried out, "*Ajeshi*, please, I have no money! I have nothing! Please, spare me sir! I have nothing of value, please!"

Frustrated and realizing that the young girl – who now appeared even younger to him close-up – was telling him the truth, the man fingered the crescent moon encircling her neck, "Hmmm, this will have to do," he whispered, his famished gaze stealing a glimpse at Sa Mi's horrified eyes, then, snapping it off of her neck without warning.

Sa Mi gasped as the leathery-faced man in white peasant clothes took steps slowly away from her, gripping her treasured necklace between his fingers, before running back down the road the way he came. Disbelieving that he was truly gone, Sa Mi stood plastered against the bark of the gingko tree, trying to see beyond her tears and the trembling of her body. After a few moments, she bent her knees until she became a tightly-wound orphan on the damp earth, her body heaving in the darkness as her hand searched in vain for a familiar jade crescent but landed instead on a fragile, frantic heart.

It seemed the wisdom of her fifteen years was not the result of a naïve disposition, but an observant insight into the human heart. It was as she had always thought: cruelty did not belong only to the Japanese. Indeed, it sprang forth from the relentless and wanton vessels of human greed and inadequacy. Only individuals were capable of allowing its existence. Only individuals were victim to it.

When Sa Mi finally emptied herself of her fear and attachments, she stood up yet again to face the same unassuming darkness of night. Steadily, she placed one foot before the other, recalling her taste of freedom just moments before, now abruptly replaced with a loneliness marked by the hollow thud of her feet striking the earth and the sounds of locusts humming in the trees.

When she finally reached her sister Ock's house Sa Mi saw a lantern glowing from the courtyard, signaling her sister's restlessness and persistent insomnia. Sa Mi leaned her forehead against the gate in relief and exhaustion as she lightly wrapped her fist against the entranceway and let out a measured, "*Eonni?*" knowing her sister was just on the other side.

"Who's there?!" her sister's sharp voice demanded, then, hearing her youngest sister's frail response, Ock flung open the gate as Sa Mi collapsed into her arms, a fever burning from her forehead and her appearance a disarray.

"*Uh muh na!*" Ock cried out in shock. "What has happened to you?" she demanded from the listless and damp body of her baby sister.

Ock, who countered the distant airs of her older sister with a direct and candid manner, was a task-master who had little tolerance for those who could not rise to her speed and dedication. Though some were of the opinion that she was at times overbearing and a little too strict and regimented with the tireless way that she organized her household, one had to admit that such commitment paved the way to virtue more effectively than sugary words and empty promises. Not wasting a moment, Ock delegated tasks to her servant to help Sa Mi out of her wet clothes and to cover her in blankets.

"With some rest, warmth, and good food you will be just fine," Ock declared to her sister's resting body as the village herbal doctor came to administer his wisdom the next morning. When her three young boys snuck in the room to steal a glimpse at their beloved aunt, Ock shooed them away and insisted that her equally attentive servant attend to her sister with diligence and care. Ock even refrained from berating her husband during Sa Mi's convalescence; she knew how her sharp tongue – when aimed at her husband – could make Sa Mi cringe.

Sa Mi's brother-in-law was not lazy given the generous standards for men his age at the time, but the vices he indulged in every now and then evoked the vicious in Sa Mi's sister. Perhaps Ock's reaction was a natural result of having grown up never witnessing her father drink to drunkenness or stay out late, for the virtuous councilman always came straight home from work every night. Sa Mi's father was as steadfast as the evening's horizon. It was from this sister that Sa Mi learned that no man would ever measure up to her honorable father.

Everyone is so harsh in their judgment of elder sister Ock because of her quick temper and biting words, but she is truthful and hard-working and why should she accept her husband's indulgences while she works to take care of everything and everyone? I shall never suffer so much in marriage, Sa Mi had declared shortly after Ock's wedding, when Sa Mi's life was orderly and predictable, held up by the two pillars of her existence.

31

When Sa Mi finally awoke on the fifth day of her sister's dedicated and watchful eye, her fever was gone and her stomach ravenous. Always prepared, Ock had the table ready with an array of nurturing food to nurse her sister back to health. Eyeing her curiously as Sa Mi inhaled spoonfuls of rice, the ever-practical, always-direct of her sisters began to address her.

"You know, things are just not going to be the same anymore with mother gone," she said cautiously, evoking only a barely visible nod from Sa Mi.

"The best way to honor our parents' legacy is to marry well and live out your years devoted to your family."

At this, Sa Mi paused and slowed her chewing in order to digest what was soon to come.

"Now, I know you don't like it, but this is the reality of things. I fear mother and father spoiled you into thinking they would live forever. Of course, we would all like for you to go to school, but we have our own families to think about as well. So, your other sisters and I have discussed it and we are all willing to pitch-in to marry you to a nice boy from a family of good standing. In fact, I know of someone…"

But before she could finish, Sa Mi put down her spoon, stopped chewing the spoonful of rice in her mouth, and stared down into the endless abyss of her bowl. Her studies at that moment were far from her mind, but marriage was not anywhere in the landscape. She felt abandoned by her family once again. Sa Mi reached her hand to her chest as she often did to clutch her jade pendant but found only her exposed heart.

"I know you don't like it, but there's no other way, and that is the truth of the matter." Though direct in her speech, Ock could not hide her affection for her youngest sister. She then stood up and resumed her family duties and tended to her children, all the while administering herbal concoctions so that Sa Mi could fully recover. When her husband came home late again that evening, Sa Mi lied awake as Ock's shouts made the rice paper on the door flutter in fear.

By the time the sun's rays had stretched into the crevices of the home, Sa Mi was gone. Thanks to her sister's care, the rosiness of her cheeks had finally begun to return. She looked up at the sky to see the three-quarter moon staring down at her as she walked to her sister Heebin's home. No longer clouded by the heat of fever nor by the fear of the unknown, Sa Mi took certain and deliberate steps toward her destiny. Her fate lied squarely in the hands of Heebin now, the quiet outlier of all her sisters, the gifted musician, the one who married for love and who, more than anyone, encouraged Sa Mi's scholarship. There was no place left for Sa Mi to go. As the sun continued its rapid ascent into the new day and the moon hearkened to her from a distance, Sa Mi eased herself into the cruel, caprice of the universe.

Mighty Fate

I f there was something that Heebin could do to save her
younger sister from the ill fates of marriage, from the
uncertainty of the times, indeed, from the perils of the world,
she would have done so with the same exacting determination
with which she pounded out Brahms on the bruised, but proud
Steinway that saw her into adolescence and followed her to her
matrimonial home.

Unlike her sisters for whom domesticity had a numbing
effect, with the help of her Steinway, Heebin was able to escape
the anxiety of married life by offering lessons to the young
children of Japanese expatriates, thereby earning an income of her
own. Much to the chagrin of her mother-in-law, who considered
such acts not only unpatriotic, but the exchange of money for art
no better than prostitution, Heebin endured more than her share
of abuse in order to experience such small freedoms.

Her husband, who was caught between the woman who
birthed him (and all the obligation that act engendered) and the
woman he fell in love with (and all the abuse he endured for the
vanity and arrogance of such an act), was no help in the matter.
After failed attempts of trying to pacify his mother into seeing the
merits of his beloved's vocation, (she could see none after seeking
and finding no sympathy during her own pained years of being a

34

young bride), Jin then appealed to his wife, proposing that perhaps the innocuous piano lessons left the impression with some of concession, even sympathy with the oppressors. At the suggestion that her engagement with music was of the political nature, Heebin retorted, "But my darling, music is for everyone. And like math, children should not be deprived of it, no matter what their situation or happenstance."

Jin, who was a mathematical genius, drew a clear line between the abstractions of his field of study and the pragmatic demands of life. He simply shrugged his shoulders and mumbled, "Sometimes our principles must take a subordinate role to preserve the peace in the short-term. Regardless of your intention, your act may be interpreted as a political one."

"Whoever believes that my teaching musical scales to five-year-olds is a political act may continue to think so, for such a person is not searching for the preservation of peace, but to upend turbulence," Heebin replied steadily.

Jin simply shook his head and adjusted the collar on his shirt before reaching for his briefcase to start his day at the secondary boy's school. Though he had fallen in love with his wife for her self-possessed nature, the tension between his wife and his mother had grown wearisome. As charming as his wife's headstrong nature was to him during the passionate years of their courtship, as the head of his household he found her opposition to be one of bullish obstinacy. With the unexpected visit from his sister-in-law, the past few weeks had an added strain.

Sa Mi, who had become a fixture to the couple's three young daughters, found solace in the loving eyes of her three nieces who flooded their beloved aunt with so much love and affection, for the first time since her mother's death Sa Mi found her laugh and joy recovered through the simple and unadulterated acts of childhood. With their help, Sa Mi's days quickly fell into a therapeutic rhythm of realizing her talents in the kitchen, (the years of observing her mother's cooking had apparently been the finest education), entertaining the children, and taking a moment to review her brother-in-law's books, for Jin shared her love for the mystery of numbers. The days offered her enough joy and distraction to notice but not to dwell on her sister's mother-in-law's goading disposition and Heebin's quiet and deep resistance. Her brother-in-law appeared to lack the fortitude to deal with the pressures and often retired to his room after working late and having his dinner.

Heebin, who had grown to accept the fleeting nature of romance and Society's vise grip on women cursed by talent and intelligence, fought the impulse to walk away from everything. Surprised and ashamed by the extent of her detachment and unhappiness, she found that the only remedy for her soul was to spend time summoning Beethoven and banging away on her Steinway. As bold as her private thoughts were in imagining an alternate reality for herself, she knew that for her sister, marriage was the only shelter now that their parents were dead and gone. Heebin took care to consider how to make the best out of a tragic situation, and unlike her sisters who offered Sa Mi up to the first eligible male brought to mind, Heebin discriminated based on her own experiences.

For one, Heebin thought, the absence of a mother-in-law would eliminate a whole host of budding conflict. Next, whether or not the potential in-laws were still alive, Heebin knew first-hand the power and authority of marrying someone who was first-born was not worth the obligation. Heebin would silently stand by as each one of her husband's family members appealed to Jin as the oldest son. With nothing but a meager inheritance to back up an aristocratic name, it seemed that the couple were more like the village fools than its elders so frequently were they satiating outstretched hands while barely able to meet their own obligations.

This led to Heebin's third requirement for the future mate of her baby sister to have both a title and ample resources at his disposal. Heebin guiltily dwelled on these thoughts while watching her youngest sister play with her daughters. Sa Mi appeared to her as one of the children, so young and naïve she was, and as good a situation Heebin could find for Sa Mi, she felt that the milestone of marriage for a young girl was a cruel way to usurp the small freedoms of childhood.

What Heebin could not see were her own emotions mirrored in Sa Mi. As Heebin pondered the fate of her youngest sister, Sa Mi scrutinized the sister whom she admired so deeply. Sa Mi's parents had nurtured Heebin's talents with great care, and it was painful for Sa Mi to see her sister hold so fast and desperately to the Steinway that had brought light and life to their childhood home.

The brother-in-law who Sa Mi had once adored for the joy he brought to her sister's face had become domineering in the way that privileged boys who only know incessant coddling do when they grow up without any resources to cushion failure or disappointment. The maternal resoluteness of his wife, which he once found to be so endearing, now carved a sharp grey glint in Jin's eyes and propelled him to withdraw. Sa Mi learned from her observations of Jin and Heebin about the swift and surprising ways in which people change. She learned she shouldn't be surprised by anyone's capacity to change, for better or for worse. (The "better" she had deduced, the "worse" she had witnessed many times first-hand.) There was perhaps no better example of this dynamic than her brother-in-law himself, who went from a passionate, idealistic, and inspired teacher of mathematics to a bored, complacent, and gloom of a husband.

Even sweet Heebin, who defied everyone to marry for love suffers under the grip of her cruel mother-in-law and a far different character than the one she wed. It seems there is no escape from the misery of marriage, Sa Mi observed as she tended to the garden in her sister's courtyard.

Indeed, it wasn't until after the couple had been living as husband and wife that the once tender and sensitive attention of Heebin's husband evolved into a shadowed grip of jealousy, causing Heebin to retreat into the solitude of her piano. It was no secret that Heebin was a good-looking woman. Not beautiful in the way that the youngest daughter of the family was – in the feminine way of the blossoming rose Sa Mi - but handsome (if a woman could be called that), like a sturdy calla lily.

Nobody knew this better than her husband, but this fact, while attracting him to her in the first place, drove him to exercise a control he took as a right. It seemed that Heebin's modesty and virtue as a woman was constantly being called into question; the selection of her lip color, the bend of her curls, the angle of the lapel of her shirt, were all subjects that Jin broached with an air of entitlement, as if he had authority over the motivations of his wife.

Sa Mi thought the topics her brother-in-law saw fit to mention were ridiculous, but bit her tongue in his presence, knowing that it was his charity that had granted her some semblance of normalcy. Instead, during rare, private moments with her sister, Sa Mi sought to encourage the depth and sincerity of Heebin's musical compositions, while acknowledging the stiff opposition of her mother-in-law, and the silliness of Jin's preoccupations. More than anything, she wanted her sister to stay firm in the position of her heart and convictions, and not fall sway to the opposition that surrounded her, compressing her into nothingness or causing her to break, alas, as many women before her.

"Brother-in-law and his mother are so fortunate to have inherited a virtuoso into their home. I don't know that mother and father ever recovered after you wed. 'The silence is deafening,' mother would say. And father would close his eyes and say that he was listening to you play from memory. He said he heard every note."

"Hmm," Heebin replied, "I don't know that mother-in-law would know a virtuoso if Chopin played beside her. She does not care for such things my darling. You will find as you go on in life that mother and father were quite rare in their values and dispositions. They brought us up in unlikely circumstances."

Though Sa Mi usually liked how Heebin used affectionate terms like, "my darling" when she addressed her, now that she was on the precipice of womanhood she couldn't help feeling an air of condescension in her sister's voice. It was an adult conversation that Sa Mi was attempting to broach, a sisterly one like she had heard all three of her older sisters engage in from time-to-time. But try as she might, there was no escape to Sa Mi's status of being the baby. Her sisters' treatment of her only affirmed her decision not to disclose her encounter with the drunk in the middle of the night. They would only chastise her as if she was still a child now that her parents were gone.

Noting her sister's silence, Heebin set down the embroidery she was working on and smiled. She reached for her sister's hand and summoned the speech she had rehearsed ever since she received the letter from the esteemed Yi *saboneem* just two days earlier. The news was fortuitous. The landlord's second son fit all of Heebin's criteria for a husband for her sister. The prospect of marrying Sa Mi to landlord Yi's youngest son far outshined any other proposals set forth by her sisters. Heebin wanted only the very best for her baby sister, and because marriage was the remedy to Sa Mi's orphaned state, she could ensure only that her baby sister would marry well.

"I have wonderful news," she started, perking Sa Mi's eager ears. "You may recall the honorable Yi *saboneem*, who is an old friend of our parents. He is in the next village over and has managed good relations with the Japanese oversight and has retained much of his rich and expansive land."

Sa Mi shook her head slightly, indicating that she did not recall such a friend. Due to her father's position, they had often hosted friends and extended family. It was difficult to keep everyone straight in one's mind.

"Yi *saboneem* has two sons, the younger of whom is only eighteen."

Heebin had barely gotten the sentence out of her mouth before Sa Mi knew where she was headed. The thought that her beloved Heebin was also impatient to send Sa Mi off and to see her enter into what even Heebin experienced as a shroud of disappointment prevented Sa Mi from listening further. She felt a cloud descend upon her sister's words and caught only bits and pieces though she noticed Heebin's mouth moving enthusiastically. "Married!" She heard her cry out, "In months' time," "Go at once to meet with the honorable home," "An end to uncertainty and mournfulness…" The phrases bounced back and forth before Heebin clasped her hands together and stood up, satisfied that she had effectively communicated the glory of the occasion.

After the news of the magnificent Sun Yi had distracted the household from its daily pressures and anxieties, Sa Mi quietly retired to her room that evening. She packed up her things, folded her blankets and assembled her scant belongings into her *podegi* as she had done so many times before, her leaky faucet of tears marking a path of her movements. Sa Mi then slipped out the front door where she was greeted by a faithful full moon. It wasn't until she was outside that she allowed herself to wail, allowed all that was inside of her to be released into the light of the moon.

There Sa Mi lay. On a cold patch of grass underneath a pair of shooting stars and a watchful moon. There she lay, the memory of a lonely jade pendant wrapped around her soul and a night silence enveloping her in darkness; the spirit of her dead parents watching helplessly from above.

There was nowhere else to go had she had any gasps of air left inside of her. Instead, as Sa Mi's tears penetrated the earth, she resigned herself to Fate's inexorable resolve. Indeed, if that mighty axe ever came grinding down on her (as she surmised it surely would in her tender, though wise sixteenth year under the stars), she would simply step aside.

Sa Mi, beloved *mangnae*, born in the year of the metal ox. No longer a little girl, but a young woman staring into her destiny. A lonely jade pendant pierced into her heart.

Meet the Groom

In a neighboring village

Yi Sun Soo was a typical *yangban* son of his time. He filled what he could not receive in love and affection with the vices that were available to him through his wealth and privilege. With all the filial responsibility left to his older brother, Sun had that much more time to idle his energies and talents. Though he was able to focus his attentions every now and then to produce profound verses of poetry in his exacting and delicate script, the majority of his time was spent indulging in the best of the best, whether it was wine, women, or the lavish affairs that men of his stature often enjoyed.

Since his mother had died when he was barely an adolescent, there was all the more reason to fill the dark void in his heart with excesses. She was the one nurturing presence in his life. But try as he might, there were not enough gambling halls (his vice of choice) on the Korean peninsula to satiate one-tenth of the *han* that cloaked his soul like a muddy abyss.

After all, he was not his brother. He had the unfortunate duty of being born second; that is, to remain in the shadow of his older brother. Sun's respect for tradition compelled him to honor this tradition, though his God-given talents illuminated his presence wherever he set foot. He was, indeed, the far better-looking of the two brothers, having inherited his mother's flawless skin and chiseled bone structure. The affect his attractive face had on a set of eyes combined with his quick wit and humor, made him a widely-loved personality throughout the village.

Despite his charisma which drew people from all walks of life near him, it was his older brother who Sun's father groomed for a life in politics. In addition to being first-born, Intaek did not have the liability that a pretty face can be in a political race. While appealing to the eyes, good looks have no business in governance, they are hard to trust and scandal follows them everywhere.

This is why Sun sought to quell his ambitions and defer to the cards that mighty Fate had dealt to him: it was he who people loved, it would be his brother who they would answer to.

Sun accepted this fact in the same way that he resigned himself to the cool detachment of his father, for he always had the love of his mother to lean on. His father, though a respected man, was expedient in his endeavors, especially when it came to the rearing of his two boys. When their mother died Sun's father simply acquired another wife to fulfill the household duties. Sun's brother took after him in many ways.

Sun felt like a stranger in their presence.

The close bond that anchored him to his family had all but died with his mother. Sun never felt understood by his distant father or his ineffectual brother. Instead, he kept the fire coursing through his veins to himself and aimed to steer clear from both of their disparaging gazes.

It was not that the distinguished patriarch was disinterested, the successful landowner simply had many more important things on his mind. He passed many days without speaking a word to his youngest son, for there was always business to discuss with the oldest. Over the years, Sun's bitterness toward his father became a rancor aimed at his own self. He could not distinguish the feelings that his father felt for him from what he told himself in his moments of loneliness.

At least the father of the two sons was aware enough of the happenings in his household to know when to step-in and to send his youngest son to marriage. By then the whole town was wise to the fact that Sun had fallen prey to the seductions of a popular girl in the neighborhood who was elevated to fame for two reasons: The first reason had little to do with her at all, for the coincidence of her birth, like all miracles, was sheer fate.

She was daughter to the wealthiest man in the village and for miles surrounding the Cholla-namdo province. Sun's father did business with this man who was small in stature and disposition, but plump in his capacity for good fortune, particularly when it came to money. He was not a very well-educated man, but everything the portly Chu laid a finger on seemed to turn to gold. One would not recognize him as the wealthiest man in the province for his dress and appearance betrayed this fact as he shoved the piles of money he made to his sticky-palmed wife and their one and only daughter. Unfortunately for Chu, his good fortune in business was paralleled by the hard luck in his personal life. And like all streaks of luck, his fortune in business was soon drained by the diseases of his home.

People knew little about the fresh-faced wife the portly Chu brought back home one day, years ago from a trip to Pusan. Rumors flew that he had plucked her from a *kisaeng* house or acquired her from a business deal with her destitute parents. Either story was believable given the man's soft heart when it came to saving young, helpless things. As rich as Chu was, it was said that if all else failed he could always make a living nursing young animals back to health. He had a penchant for rescuing wounded animals. Unfortunately, Chu's veterinary skills did not prove successful in his home and he was not as fortunate with his wife.

Once demure and soft-spoken, a delicate young thing that gossip could not sustain, her round features soon became jagged, and she did not leave the house unless she was covered in only the best of textiles and jewels, though her husband looked like a pauper. When wives began to notice their husbands exchanging familiar glances with this woman, she became the she-devil of the village, but none of their vicious words or vindictive stares could penetrate the opium eyes of that town poison.

Together the couple shared a daughter whose second reason for fame was both a matter of inheritance as well as a recognition all her own. She inherited nothing from the portly Chu, and if it ever bothered him that she was not truly his he never showed it. Although daughters often take after their mothers, Meeyoung was a star in her own right. While her mother conducted her affairs with the sleekness of a tigress, Meeyoung was like a wild horse in her unabashed manner of seeking out the young *yangban* boys and making men out of them. While her mother would not condescend to admit anything to anybody or show that the ugly words around her bothered her in the slightest, Meeyoung was of the disposition to tell one in their face with a show of pride. It was with this arrogance that she began to spread the word that she had fallen in love with the younger Yi boy and would soon be his wife.

Now, it was true that the younger Yi boy did return her affections, but as hot a fever that the girl gave his eighteen-year-old sensibilities, he never made any promises to her and knew that a future between them would never be possible, though she began to insist for one when her feelings turned soft. As a result, Sun's father helped him along in this bind and expedited the pre-wedding arrangements he had made for his youngest son. He recalled with fond memories the generosity of the future in-laws Sun would have had, had the respectable couple not met their tragic fates prematurely.

Sun's father remembered visiting the village of the councilman and being invited to his home, as was customary of local government officials and visiting landowners. He passed a pleasant evening in the honorable home and even made vague references to the ages of their children, and perhaps how someday in the future one of their children could forge a union with his own, allowing the friends to see one another more frequently. Stranger things have happened, they thought. They all received a good laugh at this idea given that the two youngest daughters of the councilman were then still in grade school.

Sun's father thanked them for their hospitality, asked them to visit him so he could return their kindness, and promised them that he would be back again in the near future. When he heard of their untimely back-to-back deaths years later, the elder Yi was at least heartened to hear that they had died having sent three out of their four daughters down the wedding aisle. He then tracked down one of those daughters to send his condolences when he realized that she lived over in the next village. Surprisingly, she wrote back to her parents' old friend, thanking him for his thoughts and relaying her concern about her youngest sister. The esteemed Yi *saboneem* wouldn't happen to know of any likely prospects? They had some dowry, not a lot, but as someone who had known her parents and could attest that they were from a respectable family, he must be able to make an appropriate recommendation?

A man of his word, the dignified landowner let the letter sit for some time as he pondered how to respond to his deceased friend's daughter's desperate inquiry.

It was a significant responsibility. The girl had pleaded to him as a surrogate family member, as a hopeful presence in the absence of her own father.

He pondered this request as his mind sifted through potential mates for the young girl: sons of mutual friends, neighbors, extended family members; however, finding a marriageable *yangban* male was always a challenge, and the young men that came to mind were no exception. He was still deep in thought one evening when he occasioned upon his youngest son who, even with his head bowed upon entering the home and encountering his father, could not hide the flush in his cheeks and the heat emanating from his veins.

"*Onyanghaseyo aboneem*," he stammered before being waved on by his father.

"This boy is an eternal puzzle to me," mused the landowner. Reflecting on the boy's meanderings throughout the town and his ease among the people, the landowner concluded, "He takes after his mother," sighing regretfully. Though his deceased wife's warmth and charm among the people elevated his status, he viewed such qualities as liabilities in his son. He was often stumped by the boy's character and disposition but acknowledged to himself that Sun had been dealt a cruel blow with the loss of his mother. He both pitied and dismissed him as the second son. In this manner he allowed the boy to seize upon a freedom that a more attentive father would not allow.

After witnessing the flush on Sun's cheeks which appeared to be a sign of merriment from alcohol and company, the father, for the first time in his life, viewed the boy as a young man. Up to that moment, it had never occurred to him that when his eldest son was Sun's age, he had already been promised in marriage. The older son had also demonstrated a maturity, a seriousness rather, that this one did not. But unlike arranging marriage as a natural succession as with his older son, at that moment, the weary landowner decided to marry off his younger son so that the boy might awaken to life's calls to responsibility and duty. Ever since he was a young child, the boy had a tendency to seek life's more effeminate comforts: music, poetry, art. In the landowner's opinion, Sun had never shown any interest in politics, nor did he contribute to his older brother's career in any significant way.

These thoughts and revelations led the patriarch to sit down to draft a response back to the daughter of his deceased friend. He spent several days starting the letter then deciding to change the language slightly here and there, then starting over again to adequately capture the honor of such a critical request. As he continued to draft this letter throughout the course of several days, news began to reach his ears about the boy's affair with the wealthy Chu's only child, the mother's reputation of whom the landlord could judge from first-hand experience. He imagined the daughter was not far behind in replicating her mother's path.

The flush on his son's cheeks and the recent developments with the Chu girl gave him the spark of inspiration he needed to finish the letter and to have it delivered to his deceased friend's daughter. With the weight of this critical responsibility before him, the dignified landowner clasped his hands. His correspondence indicated that he would like to talk to the older sister about the prospect of marrying his son to her sister, and yes, he recalled with great fondness, the honor of her now deceased parents. The landlord then summoned a servant to send word that they would like to extend an invitation to the sisters for a visit.

Little did he know that the moon's integrity and the fate of a broken-hearted young girl were at stake.

And the Other Woman: Chu Meeyoung

She was used to getting her way when it came to the *yangban* boys with whom she frolicked, but something was different about this time, something about the Yi boy tugged at her heart and made her desperate. Meeyoung tried to calm herself by staring out the window of the train where farmers, ankle deep in their flooded rice fields, were working the land with their oxen.

The handsome younger Yi boy, whom she had declared her lover, appeared as if his interest in her was beginning to wane. She was usually the one who left her beloved boys first, their mouths hanging open, their senses in a frenzy, and an unyielding desperation for her generous services to which she coldly refused as she moved on to her next victim.

This situation however, was entirely different. She felt a strange prick in her heart for her lover, especially when she noticed that his thoughts were not entirely centered on her. She was unfamiliar with the peculiar discomfort that this thing called "jealousy" invoked and she did not like it, not one bit. As her visits with him became shorter and shorter and her longing for him greater and greater, she began to spread the rumor that it was only a matter of time before they were to be husband and wife.

One morning she received a cruel taste of reality when her mother addressed her in one of her drug-induced hazes, "Meeyoung, when *are* you going to wed that lover of yours? Haven't you dragged this on long enough? Perhaps if you were more like your mother, you'd have been married by now, huh?" shaking her hips to taunt her daughter before she fell over in laughter.

Meeyoung fought back tears at the thought of her incorrigible fate. All the money in the world couldn't buy you a decent family, and it was a decent family that she needed in order to get married. She was no fool, nor was she immune to the stares and whispers that people engaged in at her expense. She just chose not to listen to them, but no matter how hard she tried she could not *choose* to keep it from hurting her. Meeyoung simply swallowed back her pain and the image of her opium-induced mother as she had done so many times before and devised a plan.

She was not naïve to the ways of the world and knew that what she and the younger Yi boy were doing behind closed doors was the raw act of baby making, and yet, time after time, she was not left with any babies to speak of. The only possible way the boy's father might ever consider a marriage between them was if she was able to bear her lover a son that he could not refuse, expediting a marriage to save face for both families.

Meeyoung knew that some women were cursed with the inability to bear children and she started to panic and wonder if she was one of those unfortunate women. After all, her own mother had only given birth to her, hadn't she? Meeyoung cringed at the familiar saying that daughters generally take after their mothers. And everybody (except for her own father who chose to live in denial) knew about the opium addict's romps with different married men in the town where they lived, none of which resulted in a pregnancy. Concerned about this possibility, Meeyoung kept her ears open as she wallowed around town in her misery as an unescorted, unmarried woman (the townspeople had gotten used to seeing her around in this improper state, like an orphan or prostitute with excellent taste for finery).

She was walking past a group of older women when she overheard them discussing the miracles of a certain Dr. Hwang whose treatments of the ailments of women had become legendary even beyond his practice in Gyeongseong. When they started talking about the hundreds of women he had cured of their infertility, Meeyoung boldly stepped up to the group and asked them of the exact location of this Dr. Hwang as there was some business she would like to discuss with him. As was the typical reaction of most women toward Meeyoung, they simply paused in their conversation, glanced at her as if she was a rodent, then continued on among themselves as if they had heard nothing.

Encouraged by the news, Meeyoung did not react to the cold shoulder she received, but hurried home to send a servant to seek more information about this Dr. Hwang and his magic acupuncture needles in Gyeongseong. The servant, having been swept to the margins of society, had knowledge on everyone due to her acute powers of observation. She immediately recognized who her superior was talking about and rattled off an address to her.

Meeyoung wasted no time to send a letter to Dr. Hwang requesting his services, nor did she wait for a response nor open the one that was sent to her as she was already on a train headed for Gyeongseong. Still a couple hours short of her journey, Meeyoung anxiously wondered if there was anything she could do to make the train go faster. The unopened correspondence from the respected doctor sat at her home, stating that she come promptly at her time of 3:00pm as he always holds rigidly to his appointment schedule. Meeyoung would arrive three hours ahead of schedule. She figured that with her pockets full of cash the doctor would not refuse her, as she wanted to get back to Gwangju before it was too late the next day. Though she felt that her parents would neither notice nor care that she was gone, she left a brief note for them that she was visiting her cousin in the next village. She did have the presence of mind to take her faithful servant along who had provided her with the good doctor's address, for Meeyoung had never been outside of Gwangju, and was nervous at the idea of making the journey alone.

Meeyoung was so relieved to have her *ajumma* there with her when they got off the train and were thrust into the hustle and bustle of the nation's capital. She realized how very small and provincial her little town was and vowed one day that she would escape the grips of her dreary past and come to Gyeongseong where she could start fresh and no one would know anything about her family or her background. But first things first: she needed to get pregnant and to wed the younger Yi boy. Awed by the lights and distractions before her, Meeyoung followed her servant toward the good doctor's home who was her only hope.

A Date Is Set

By the time the revered Yi *saboneem* met with Sa Mi's sister regarding marriage prospects between his youngest son and Sa Mi, he noticed Sun's earnest affliction and that the boy was too tender-hearted to let go of his feelings for Meeyoung. By now, the boy had grown sorry and somewhat responsible for being unable to reciprocate her generosity. After all, she had mentioned marriage to him on several occasions.

The elder Yi was too pragmatic to appreciate Sun's vulnerable side and he couldn't understand how any son of his could collapse physical intimacy with that of emotions and feelings, especially when it came to an unchaste girl like Chu's daughter. (He could confirm her mother's reputation for generosity first-hand, but unlike his son he did not let his emotions get the best of him. Instead, he concealed his passions behind closed doors and left them behind after their sessions of intimacy ended.)

Had the elder Yi known that the girl was capable of doing such a number on his son, he would have put a stop to things much sooner. He had just assumed that the boy was having a little fun as sons are entitled to do every now and then. At least the boy did know that he could never marry the girl and that his affection for her was not of the enduring kind. But Sun still couldn't help feeling sorry for Meeyoung and her sad home. What kind of future would she have while he got married in the proper form? Perhaps what he felt more than anything was guilt.

While the esteemed landlord regretted every romantic notion in his son's head that compelled him to write poetry, (not of the useful political kind, but that which revered the changing of the seasons, or the fickle nature of his youthful heart), Sun continued to brood over the fate of the frisky Chu girl. It was not that the elder Yi did not appreciate such inspirations, his first wife, after all, had been a tapestry artist and created the most divine images of nature and life with needle and thread, it was just that he dreaded to see such qualities in a son. Such dramas could be endearing in a woman, but a man who was too revealing with his emotions displayed weakness, and there was no other way that he could describe his second son.

Given Sun's wandering tendencies, the elder Yi thought the best thing to do would be to marry him to the youngest daughter of the couple who had bestowed such warmth to him during one pleasant visit to their village. In this way he was doing everyone a favor. Surely the spirits of the dead couple were smiling upon him. When he saw the girl who would be his daughter-in-law, he realized just how great a favor he must be doing for her parents as anyone could see how their absence had placed a permanent wound upon her heart and a hollowness in her eyes. Noticing the older man's reaction as her sister bowed to him, Sa Mi's sister Heebin quickly stated, "She is still mourning the deaths of our parents you see, but I know that once her coveted wedding day comes closer, she will be a devoted wife who will bear you many grandsons, isn't that right Sa Mi?"

Sa Mi, no longer fighting the fickle reins of Fate – resigned as she was to the fog enveloping the path before her – simply bowed in affirmation.

"Of course," the bespectacled man replied compassionately, "hopefully having her own family will help secure the memory of her parents."

She was certainly an adorable young woman, someone who his son would find attractive, and knowing him his son would be intrigued by the bruise upon her soul, so easily moved was he. If anyone would help him forget that Chu daughter it would be this young woman before him. She came from an honest, virtuous background and looked like she could serve her husband like a proper young lady, or at least be trained to perform the tasks that were expected of her.

Though the distinguished man preferred someone who could control his son's romantic meanderings, he knew he could not put anything past anyone. He and his wife had selected his other daughter-in-law because they did not want anyone to overshadow their prize son's demeanor, but rather act as an ornament to him. Her face was serene and her demeanor soft-spoken, but to everyone's surprise, she grew into a firecracker of a woman. It took all of his first wife's energy to try and calm the blaze of her daughter-in-law's impulses and she was the cause of many headaches for his first son, loud and unruly as she was.

So, the landlord simply shrugged his shoulder on this point, because there didn't seem to be a foolproof way to predict what kind of woman the lonely child before him would grow into, other than the popular advice when seeking a daughter-in-law which was, "look toward the mother, for that is who the daughter will become." Thanks to this saying, many mothers botched their daughters' prospects in marriage due to their own questionable reputations. Because this option was not available to the elder Yi he did the next best thing and that was to meet with the girl's sister, who seemed to be doing very well in her household and had an impeccable reputation where she lived providing piano lessons to neighborhood children. That certainly showed some independence, a quality that would complement his own son's weaknesses very well. It also made him remember the controlling and dominant woman who was his first son's mother-in-law and he wondered how he could have ever been so naïve. But that was in the past, no need to think about it now. The business before him was far too pressing.

"Very well," the old man started, "I will leave it up to you to seek an auspicious date for the wedding and in the meantime, I will get everything ready on my end. It will be a glorious celebration, but please, do select the earliest date possible, it can't be too soon. My son is anxious to meet his new bride." With that Sun's father made a quick gesture toward his timid future daughter-in-law, and then started on his way. Heebin was beside herself with the wonderful news.

"Isn't that great?!" she exclaimed turning toward Sa Mi, who stared back searchingly at the sister who had so gravely disappointed her.

A changed young woman, with no other prospects and nowhere left to turn, Sa Mi then simply replied, "Yes. Yes it is." To herself she thought, *Such is the nature of adulthood: to object until the unhappiness takes its toll* (as with the case of the rebel martyrs, or her sister Heebin herself), *or to compromise until your own desires and dreams are unrecognizable* (as with the Japanese sympathizers, or her oldest sister Young with whom she felt an unlikely kinship in that moment). *Could it be that defeat was the only avenue to peace?*

"Come," Heebin said excitedly, to counter the uncertain dialogue in her sister's head, "let us go quickly to the fortune teller so she can tell us the best date for your wedding," her hand clutching a slip of paper with the birthdates of her sister and her future brother-in-law. The fortune teller would use these to make predictions based on the cosmos, as if the stars could provide any insight into the couple's future happiness and relieve everyone's anxiety for the unknown. Sa Mi followed in silence.

#

The cherry blossoms were in full bloom that year. Around the time of year when Sa Mi and her sister left the pock-marked fortune teller, the grass was covered in pink petals and the scent of azaleas was just beginning to tickle one's nose. Dragonflies were dancing among the hummingbirds and the sun lingered later and later into the day until it finally made its escape over the horizon, leaving the sky a translucent glow of scarlets, yellows, and violets. Sa Mi sat at the top of a grassy hill while a butterfly flirted with the loose tendrils of her hair. She stared out into the amber sky as if she was looking into her future and the mysteries that lie ahead.

Sa Mi was to be married in less than four months and she could no longer run from her life. The pock-marked seer had surmised that the new moon with the new harvest was an auspicious day for her to embark on her journey with the stranger that was to be her husband. All she could do was hope that she would learn to love this Sun and that he would love her in return. She knew nothing about the love between a man and a woman aside from the shouting of her sisters with their husbands late into the evening, and the humility with which her parents cooperated with each other more with action and less with words. Sa Mi had vague ideas and little interest in what her duties were during that first night she was to share with her husband. Matters like these were always cloaked in hushed whispers she overheard among her sisters, or the giggles of her now distant classmates.

How she longed to see her school friends at that moment. She imagined them to be studying between moments of laughter and gossip. Sa Mi was by far the most serious student of them all. Like her father, she could command a crowd's attention toward nobler pursuits after episodes when her classmates would speculate about forbidden topics such as one's wedding night or comment on the charm of their handsome English teacher. Sa Mi would manage to bring the group's attention back to the algebra problem they were contemplating or the meaning of a poem that they debated. All the young women respected Sa Mi's love of learning and benefited from her scholarship, though few truly shared in the belief that the pursuit of knowledge could do anything for their chartered futures.

Those days were over now and her life had taken an abrupt turn. Sa Mi knew that somewhere her parents were watching her, saddened by their untimely deaths and what their absence had done to their beloved *mangnae*. She could not let them be disappointed or disheartened anymore by her pitiful sight.

Sa Mi stared into the descending dusk. Her fist rested against her heart where her beloved jade pendant used to hang and in that moment she vowed to be her best in the new role that her future father-in-law had bestowed upon her with the complicity of her sister.

She would be somebody's wife in less than four months.

The Song of Sa Mi and Sun

Meeyoung was in terrible shape ever since she returned from her visit to Gyeungseong. Her servant tended to her and administered potions and remedies to help purge the worms and illnesses that were responsible for Meeyoung's misery. Consumed and exhausted, Meeyoung could barely pull herself out of bed, and try as *ajumma* might, she could not get her master to keep anything down. The medicine only seemed to make her feel worse.

The trip had turned out to be a complete waste of time. Upon meeting her the famous Dr. Hwang raised his eyebrows as Meeyoung prostrated herself before him and pleaded, "Please doctor, you must help me become fertile!" He then took a deep breath, offered her a cup of tea, and proceeded to tell her he could not treat her without the presence of her parents. He then gave her a five-minute lecture on the complexities of fertilization and sent her on her way, duly noting that she was a young underage girl despite her claims. To make matters worse and to add to her dejection and desperation, Meeyoung found that she was violently ill the whole ride back.

Meeyoung was still ill days after her return, and one afternoon when she was exercising her routine of purging up her insides, her mother appeared in the doorway like a serpent. Peering at her daughter she took slow, indulgent drags from a cigarette in a holder, and was dressed in a long jade-colored Western silk nightie with a fur shawl draped around her shoulders. She looked like she belonged in another world, beautiful as she was and dressed so completely inappropriate for the times. Still, Meeyoung was always awed by her mother and in her vulnerable state her hunger for her mother's attention was burning a hole inside of her. It didn't matter to her that her mother's eyes had that rancid yellow glow that obscured reality and indicated that her high was as fresh as the morning sun.

"*Omonee, omonee*..." Meeyoung groaned, "I'm sick, oh *omonee* please help me, please help me," she cried.

The elegant serpent stood in front of the rice paper screen and took a slow drag from her cigarette. Finally, she responded without moving from her position, "Poor baby, *aii uhri Meeyoung-a*, there there..."

Meeyoung's heart came alive and her blood stronger at the sound of those words, how she needed to hear them from her own mother's sweet voice, how she longed to hear them again. If she could only hear those words she would never need to seek anymore *yangban* boys underneath the sheets. She sat staring into her vomit as her mother's yellow eyes gazed down on her. Meeyoung sat patiently for more of those coveted words, for that sweet mother voice to fill her ears.

The lithe figure had almost reached the end of her cigarette when her senses came back, "There, there *uhri Meeyoung...uhdi apuh no? (Are you hurting?)*... You're not sick *uhri Meeyoung-a*," at this Meeyoung cocked her head up toward her mother, hungry for more of those honey words, but instead she heard, "*You're just a whore. Don't you see that you have a seed growing inside of you darling?"* she raised her voice ever so sweetly on this point and creased her yellow eyes compassionately toward her daughter.

At this, Meeyoung's chest began to heave and like the beginning of a tsunami, she felt tremors all throughout her body until tears started to stream down her face. She was a silent, shaking mess. And while she could not control the impending flood, she would not let her mother hear the crying wails that originated so deep within of her.

The green serpent started to shake as well but did not seek to mask her uncontrollable laughter. As the ashes of her cigarette danced in the air and her fur stole dragged along the floor, Meeyoung's mother continued to play with that incomparable feeling that the opium possessed in her, allowing her to laugh at life's woes and absurdities.

Still holding onto the wall, her yellow gaze focused in on the silent, trembling ball on the floor that was soaking the whole room in tears, the lithe figure then abruptly changed her demeanor to better match her attire.

Sharpening her eyes and pursing her lips she held out the palm of her hand and demanded, "Give me the money. I know your father gave you some money now give it to me! Give it to me!" she screamed from the doorway like a madwoman, "Give it to me you no good whore! Give it to me!" she screamed flinging her cigarette holder at the silent earthquake. Her yellow gaze now transformed into fire, she took one last glance at the ball on the floor before she flung her fur stole behind her in search of that elusive laughter that tasted so sweet. Her business was done there.

The silent ball remained on the floor, shaking and trembling like a giant crevice in the earth, falling into the black hole of nothingness.

Something happened to Meeyoung that day when her mother had apprised her of her condition. What little hope she had of marrying the Yi boy or marrying anyone for that matter had vanished, and any illusion she was under about her power over men had disappeared as well. Nobody really took her seriously. It was like her mother had said: she was nothing but a whore, no better than the girls in the slums she had heard stories about who beg for a *won* or two in exchange for their bodies. She was worse than even those girls however, since her lovers left her with nothing but their shame or contempt.

She stopped seeing the younger Yi boy, not that he continued to seek her generous company. He was too busy with the planning of his wedding. She found out about this one day when she had overheard her father telling someone what a no-good family those Yi's were for leading them on like they were going to marry Meeyoung, and then making arrangements at the last minute with someone else. The homely man probably felt the need to save face given that the whole town and anyone nearby knew that Meeyoung had quite the reputation, and that nobody would marry their sons to his daughter, nor advise any of their friends to, no matter how much dowry the wealthy man could afford. Meeyoung was not surprised by the news and decided to keep her condition a secret for as long as she could afford. She would not use her discovery as she had previously thought, (as a way in which to seal her prospects with her lover), for fear that he would reject her all the same. It had become easier to conceal her secret as the days had grown more bearable and she felt her senses returning to her as the Yi's big wedding day grew nearer and nearer. Only her mother knew Meeyoung's secret, which she kept buried behind her yellow haze of opium.

Meanwhile, the Yi family patriarch prepared the grandest of affairs for his son's marriage to the orphan girl in the next village. Sa Mi was numb during that chaotic day, when terror usually assaults a young bride's conscience. The terror had already collided into her with the death of her parents and stripped her of the typical musings of a young girl her age. So that when the wedding day came, she had no fears left, only an open wound that she did not attempt to disguise. During that endless day, she only wanted to get through the pomp and ceremony and get on with what was deemed inevitable.

"Get me more rouge," Ock demanded to no one in particular.

It was the first time since their mother's death that all four sisters were in one room without their respective husbands.

As usual, Ock had taken charge with Heebin as her accomplice. Together they fawned over the finishing touches for their youngest sister after Ock had kicked out the female attendants who had previously been serving the young bride.

"That lipstick color is all wrong!" She had exclaimed with irritation, before shooing them out of the room under the disapproving look of her oldest sister Young, who shuttled in and out, spending more time greeting guests than she did addressing her sisters.

As if on cue Heebin grabbed the rouge from the table and hurried toward her sister Ock. She had just returned from playing some melodies on the piano as guests filed into the estate.

Ock and Heebin saw fit to put the finishing touches on Sa Mi and to pass on the womanly advice that gets filtered through generations.

"This is a sacred day for you," started Heebin tentatively, "you have a whole new life ahead of you."

"Remember, after all this is over you will be part of his family, in a new home," scrutinizing Sa Mi's reflection in the mirror Ock continued, "You must earn your place there, you can't let them walk all over you… Girls! Keep it down over there!" she shouted across the room at Sa Mi's nieces who were playing and laughing in front of the mirror themselves, excited about the

63

special occasion. Immune to their mother's loud and abrupt voice, they carried on.

"That's right, you must find something of yourself in the household, something that the others can't touch," Heebin added.

Sa Mi was surprised to hear her sisters' advice. She had expected them to preach the refrain about being an obedient wife and following the will of her husband. Instead they were advising her to assert herself and to find her own identity among her new roles in the house. This, from the two sisters whom Sa Mi admired the most, but whose unhappiness and disillusionment were so palpable during her time with them. Young, who had not said much all day, could not see fit to stay quiet any longer.

"What your sisters mean, I believe, Sa Mi-ya, is that harmony is best preserved when your actions satisfy your husband and his family. *You* are actually the empowered one to bring prosperity to the family home if it is a peaceful household that you seek, which ought to be our aim as wives and mothers," she finished looking at Ock and Heebin disapprovingly, who absorbed themselves further in the preening of their baby sister.

Not wanting to betray her sisters, Sa Mi nodded her head in silence.

After a brief pause, Heebin started, "Older sister is right, Sa Mi. Sometimes you may find your station at odds with the more expeditious path to harmony. Marriage is about compromise. To always be in opposition to one's plight is to always be..."

"...lonely," Sa Mi finished her sentence, her face without expression.

"Why, yes," Heebin replied to Sa Mi's expression in the mirror. "Lonely."

The surprise in Heebin's tone reminded Sa Mi that each of her sisters was experiencing their own personal turmoil and coming to terms with what their lives had become. Young was no different from Heebin and Ock in this, and it wasn't until that very moment that Sa Mi realized that she might have unfairly judged her.

Ock interrupted her thoughts, "Well, we are all in agreement that you will be far better positioned than all of us without a mother-in-law to satisfy."

"You can count on that," Heebin echoed, perhaps more eagerly than she had intended. "That new wife of *Yi saboneem* hardly counts as a mother-in-law, it is clear she wields little power in that household."

The sisters, absorbed in their own reflections on marriage, and ambivalent to what fate they were sending their youngest and most-loved sister, spent the rest of the time anxiously fussing over Sa Mi. What was left unsaid clung to the air like a dense fog. The occasion called into question the sisters' uncertainties of pushing their orphaned sister into marriage. Everyone knew the fate of young orphan girls who have been sold into marriage; they become no better than glorified servants who are at the mercy of their in-laws. As good a match as it might have been, the sisters' words stood in stark contrast to the reality before them.

Nevertheless, everyone did their share to make sure that the event and attendant proprieties were carried out properly and with care. Sa Mi herself, no longer objected to her fate, but observed her new family intently. Even in her most critical posture, she could find few faults in her father-in-law who doted on her affectionately, though he was generally restrained with his emotions with everyone else. Sun, who was but three years her senior did not look her way much at all, and the fact that he appeared to be as confused and unhappy with the contrived affair endeared her to him. They were approaching the union with the same blank expectation and resignation. Sa Mi could also not help taking note of the undertone of sadness obscured by Sun's wit and charm among the guests, it was a solitude that Sa Mi recognized in herself. *After all,* Sa Mi thought to herself, *he also knows the pain of losing his own mother.*

It was not long before the memories of her wedding day and the days and weeks following it were a giant grey mass in Sa Mi's heart. Everything had happened so quickly and her new life took over, distancing herself from the childhood where she sought shelter before her parents departed from the earth.

Unlike for most women who cry themselves to sleep every night trying to adjust to the labors of marriage, Sa Mi had already cried all her tears away and thanks to the generosity of her father-in-law, had few labors to worry about. There were servants to attend to the chores of the household and though she was spared the taxing and mundane daily work of the home, her status in the house charged her with the responsibility of ensuring that everything was up to standard. She poured her heart into the details that transform a dwelling into a home and her taste for perfection was reflected in the sparkle of the silverware and the smooth starchiness of the linen. Her tight-lipped mother-in-law who became irritated with her husband's affections toward the girl, asserted her authority when she could, though she could not ultimately contend with the favor that Sa Mi enjoyed among her new family and the servants. Instead, the older woman was limited to baseless criticisms when her husband and stepson were out of earshot. The rest of the time, she busied herself with keeping up her appearance, and therefore left Sa Mi alone.

Through her new role, Sa Mi was able to develop her excellent cooking skills. She became an expert at seasoning the spicy stews that her husband fervently devoured and fermenting the *kimchi* precisely to his liking. Sun's controlled affections and momentary brooding during those first few months of marriage did not concern her but gave her time to get used to the idea of consummating their marriage and relieved her of the stress that she heard other women describe about the fumbling, awkward, and even painful experience of their wedding nights and the expectations that were harbored soon thereafter.

Sa Mi didn't know of the object of Sun's fits of solemnity, only that her cooking seemed to comfort him and awaken his appetite. Despite his moodiness, it was obvious that he could not hide his attraction for her as she caught him more than once watching her with a guarded curiosity. She had been loved too much by her own parents to question whether her new husband would love her. Her parents' devotion to her instilled a confidence that she was always worthy of love. This led her to believe that his sad fog would eventually melt away, and she surprised herself when she found that she was vested in his happiness. Perhaps he was thinking about his own deceased mother in the same way that the memories of her own parents tugged at her heart every night before she fell asleep.

While her husband sought to shelter his loneliness among poetry and vice, Sa Mi sought to ease her pain through song. Every night before going to bed, Sa Mi would steal a few moments to sing to herself and to allow her sorrows to be carried away by her angelic voice. She did not realize it when one night her husband came home early to catch her in the act of singing. Embarrassed, she stopped abruptly and bowed her head. The young man was shocked at the sound that escaped her – as if the sky itself could open up and breathe – as if the most breathtaking sunset had its own melody – for this was the sound of Sa Mi's voice, that of angels. Sun begged her to continue and fell weak at each note she hit precisely, striking every chord of his heart. It was as if she had reached into his soul and plucked the strings of his solitude one by one.

This is how the younger Yi boy began forgetting about his amorous affections for Meeyoung and began allowing his heart to open up to his new wife. This is how their true love affair began, well into their marriage, to the tune of Sa Mi's heavenly voice.

Enter Soonjin

As with any inconvenient truth, the maxim: "In order to learn about the daughter, one must look toward the mother," is accurate when it is applied to others and not oneself. The idea that we are born into this existence inheriting characteristics other than the more obvious physical traits from our mothers is objectionable on many levels. After all, to be held to the saintly attributes or to be limited by the questionable reputations of one's mother is far too narrow and dubious to be enumerated here.

Perhaps what is closer to the truth is the way in which acceptance of this maxim had carved its place as indisputable fact in the hearts of many. The imposition of this maxim to daughters everywhere on the Korean peninsula served to affirm the rule, rather than contradict it, so that the quiet daughter of the unruly mother was really a devil inside, and the rebellious daughter of the reserved mother would soon quiet her passions.

Applying this maxim to Meeyoung was far too obvious an affirmation of its truth that people everywhere used it as a living example to support the declaration that daughters take after their mothers, as in: "Just look at the Chu girl and her mother! That girl is destined to follow in her mother's footsteps!"

Meeyoung, however, saw nothing similar between the identity she embodied and that remote, languid soul that was her mother. The desperations that were at the core of her being and that motivated every one of her actions were nowhere to be found in her mother, whose cool detachment was downright frightening at times. Meeyoung, who made every excuse for the mother with whom she was inextricably bound, solemnly vowed never to go near that sticky, yellow heaven her mother loved so dearly, and on which she squarely placed the blame for her mother's maternal shortcomings.

In fact, Meeyoung did keep her vow to stay away from the opium her mother so adored. After all, it was the opium that accompanied her mother to darkness like a loyal friend one rainy night when Meeyoung was in her eighth month, tossing, turning, and sweating in her sleep.

Meeyoung woke up to the screams of her father and went into her parents' room to find her mother's beautiful face an ashen gray, a crushing silence surrounding her very form. And yet, a sense of peace emanated from her mother's image that had eluded her in her living years, captivating Meeyoung and compelling her to stare at her mother for what seemed like frozen time. She did not notice nor hear her father's cries or that of the servants rushing back and forth in a panic. Meeyoung simply stared at what remained of her mother: a beauty the opium could not rob, a stubborn beauty, and a beauty that was so utterly useless.

Before long, the scene before her turned into streaks of light against a velvet background, surreal and intangible. Meeyoung fainted.

When she awoke from her dream she found herself in a hospital with an IV of sweet liquid hooked up to her arm. *Morphine*, she saw the nurse mouth to her in her stupor. In her haze Meeyoung thought she saw another nurse walking toward her with a bundle in her arms, but before she reached her,

Meeyoung closed her eyes, the sweet liquid in her arm filtering her lonely vision.

Her recovery was wrought with stabbing pains which she quelled with this new discovery – *morphine* – the anodyne that helped to ease her incessant suffering. When she felt the pain coming on, or saw images of her mother's ashen face, she would begin her cries for the drug and if the servants were not quick enough, these cries eventually turned into screams and violent tremors that terrorized everyone around her. As the days and weeks fluttered past her in a confusing daze, Meeyoung found she needed more and more of the morphine as she watched the nursing and care of her infant girl from a distance. It was obvious to everyone that the baby had inherited that useless beauty that belonged to her grandmother. One could also see the baby girl's resemblance to her father which emphasized her proud face even further.

Meeyoung could barely stand to look at the infant girl and her deep, round eyes that she had inherited from her father. Her cherubic face was too bitter of a reminder of the heartache Meeyoung thought she would never suffer fooling around with that Yi boy. He was now a husband to some poor naïve girl from a neighboring town. What could Meeyoung do with the pathetic bundle before her? Word had already spread all over town about her newest and most enduring love affair with that dream-inducing heaven that washed her memories away. Her father was losing money by the day as workers stole from him in his broken, catatonic stupor.

The stocky man had never conceived that his lovely wife could ever fall into Death's greedy arms. The opium was part of her existence and had been for many years, she knew exactly how to use it, how to control it, and when it was too much. In his deepest illusions, he never thought it would kill her. The aging man was not the least bit heartened by the birth of his only grandchild, especially given the humiliating circumstances of her conception. And he was too preoccupied to know what everyone else knew about his daughter's newest love affair with morphine; he simply thought she was still recovering from her trauma. And to be honest, he didn't much care. He figured that this was the way of women, to fade into the shadows of the home, and to disappear one day without warning.

And so it was. As to not disappoint her father's conception of the opposite sex, Meeyoung followed the same pattern as her own despaired mother. She awoke one morning before the sun, packed up every trace of drug she could find, wrapped her daughter in a blanket, and placed her in a bassinet. Meeyoung walked out of the estate without looking over her shoulder and headed straight to the Yi estate across the way.

She entered through the courtyard, the world still in slumber with the only sounds of the well water dripping steadily from the bucket and the crickets finishing their nighttime sonata. Meeyoung reached the front door and placed the bassinet on the front step, her baby still sleeping peacefully in her blanket. She wrote a quick note and tucked it inside the blanket. Taking one last glance at the angel face, she then turned away toward the train station.

It was the baby's father, followed by Sa Mi, who lifted the piece of paper from the bassinet. Sun was already on his way out, but servants had rushed him toward the front of the estate to view their discovery. Of course, he knew who she was after one look at her angel face which was by then cloaked in tears, her expression cold and alone. The note confirmed it: "She's yours. Take her."

This is how Sun's first child entered the household: during the tumultuous year of the tiger to the tune of a cricket sonata, her birth mother on a train to Gyeongseong, searching for her next fix.

After some deliberation the sobered father said, "Her name will be Soonjin," bowing his head to hide the despair for his only child, "She is a Yi," he said as a declaration to his young wife who had no say in the matter, only her first stinging realization of the pain of marriage, and yet another affirmation that no man would compare to her noble father.

"I will raise her as my own," Sa Mi responded, knowing her role and the convention of the times which left little room for any other response, though inside she was fighting the longing for the scent of her own deceased mother. Lifting the crying bundle Sa Mi looked down to see that she was indeed, a Yi after all. Looking at her, she finally realized the source of her husband's detachment and sorrow at the beginning of their marriage, as it returned to his face at the sight of his daughter. Words were not necessary. He bowed his head once more and left the room. Sa Mi handed the bundle to a servant.

Then Sa Mi retreated to her room, closed the rice paper screen, and sang from the depths of her very being, tears covering her eyes like glass, her young heart opened to her new husband, only to be tarnished by the crying baby in the next room.

Life was a study in the annihilation of illusions. The most private, sacred space she had shared with him, the texture of the moments that she had begun to feel for him, he had already felt before with someone else. She was all alone with her song. Her husband did not enter the room this time.

PART II: CHILDREN

*One-by-one they arrived
and multiplied,
their catalog of needs
Ablaze behind wet, storied eyes.
Desperate for love
and ready to bestow it.*

Sa Mi Settles In

Ever since the tiny bundle was left at her doorstep, Sa Mi tried to care for the rosy-cheeked emblem of her husband's love for another. But even with her most generous heart, she often found that the sight of the babe evoked a sadness in her, and she quickly handed her off to a servant.

It seemed that ever since the baby arrived Sa Mi felt ill and weak at the knees, the world spinning viciously before her eyes. Trying in vain to fend off her nausea, Sa Mi felt as she had swallowed a ball of lead that was rolling back and forth inside her tiny belly. Her husband, feeling a pang of guilt at the sight of his new bride, flooded her with nurses, maids, and jewels to try and ease her discomfort.

The arrival of the baby had collapsed Sa Mi's childlike illusions and she nursed the wound that had replaced the innocent love she felt for Sun. As was her nature for the few she had loved in her life, including the parents that peered at her through the night sky, Sa Mi worshipped Sun from a distance and within the safe confines of her heart. She noted Sun's concern for her, but even her pride couldn't control the tide in her belly that compelled her to hover over the chamber pot.

75

When her condition continued on from days to weeks, Sa Mi realized that a baby of her own was forming inside her belly. After hearing the news, her protective father-in-law demanded that the servants take over the care of the baby girl completely and that his daughter-in-law not lift a finger lest she disturb his legitimate grandchild. Sa Mi conceded to this demand as the forming baby inside of her caused her such sleepiness and fatigue, she found she could barely get out of bed.

Meanwhile, the baby Soonjin was quite a handful in the household and cried like she was grieving her own mother. She thought the louder she cried, the more likely her mother would return for her, but no matter how much she tried, Soon saw only unfamiliar faces around her. It didn't matter that her own mother treated her like a stranger the few weeks that she had known her. Soon still yearned for that figure on the other side of the umbilical cord like a baby serpent pines for its mother after she abandons her to the dark and unpredictable currents of existence. Soon was somewhat satiated when her father would hold her, but these episodes were few and far between, as men simply did not hold children back in those days. It was the sentimentality of his heart that drove him to betray tradition, and sheer boredom that compelled Sun to return Soon to the nursemaid's arms after only a few minutes.

Besides, Sun was restless, and not one to linger around the home much. He respected his wife and made sure that she was well cared for, but sometimes wished she was more demonstrative with her feelings. Not too much though, his independent spirit would not be able to tolerate a wife that was too sticky on him. But Sun did crave attention and wondered whether Sa Mi was still angry at him over the crying bundle that was left at their doorstep one still morning. No matter, he really couldn't complain, she never asked where he was going or where he had been, and always treated him with loving respect when he returned. What more could he ask for?

Marriage however, did not put a brake on his one beloved vice: gambling. This vice combined with his taste for fine wine and his inclination to be generous with his time and money was a dangerous combination, especially because he was not often on the winning side of the game. Nevertheless, whatever affection he craved at home, he was showered with when he stepped outside the house. People loved him and everybody knew him. His father began to acknowledge his popularity among the people which had the positive effect of drawing attention to his elder brother. Sun's wit and charisma were legendary in the teahouses and *kisaeng* houses in the region, where other privileged men like him congregated.

Sun was the life of the party among his friends and the proprietors of the establishments he frequented eagerly awaited his arrival. For all the others who caught a glimpse of Sun, his magnetic spirit left them wanting more of him. Everyone deferred to that distant figure who was his brother, simply due to the fact that he shared the same blood as the venerable and charming Yi Sun Soo. Fortunately, Sun had ample resources during these years which allowed him to keep the pockets of the local Japanese officials full while maintaining his lifestyle. Typical of young men blessed with the good fortune of birthright, Sun basked in his entitlement with a naïve and thoughtless sensibility.

On this particular day he was in especially good spirits after visiting with members of the township and taking a moment to reflect on his good fortune. While it was true there was a baby crying for her mother at his home, given the stories that had reached his ears about Meeyoung, Sun felt grateful that his father had helped him to dodge a bullet. If he let himself, Sun felt a prick of guilt here and there, so instead, he focused his thoughts on his beautiful wife and the fact that Sa Mi would soon bear his first legitimate heir. He knew it was going to be a boy, poised to enter the world in the year of the boar.

The thought of his soon-to-be born first son made Sun beam inside, and his high spirits sparked him to buy another round of *soju* for his friends and compatriots at the *tabang*. *Mansei!* he cried out, lifting his glass. *Good health and prosperity to all!* As he felt the heat of the *soju* roll onto his tongue, he would not allow himself to think of the fate of the mother of the crying baby girl at his home. Just as quickly as the heat of passion comes roaring into one's heart, so just as easily does it extinguish. He supposed this was just the nature of things. He hadn't thought much at all about Meeyoung the past couple months, or the playful romps they shared that now made him a father. He was a man now. He had his own family to think about. After all, he was at that ripe, wise age of twenty-one.

As the rumble in her belly began to subside, Sa Mi grew lonely in that sprawling estate surrounded by dutiful servants and the overbearing concern of her father-in-law. Though she feigned attention toward her husband's baby, she was saved from changing diapers or participating in any other acts that could potentially pollute her unborn. This undoubtedly included feeding, changing, and bathing the child whose tears had no beginning and no end, or all the daily chores and tasks that build an indelible bond between mother and child and solidify their unending dependence on each other. This was simply the consequence of her social status, and one for which she was thankful, because she could not oblige herself to care for the child her husband fathered in any kind of maternal way.

It wasn't until Sa Mi would give birth to her eighth and final child that she would come to know the power of such loving acts of motherhood. It was perhaps because she was forced to perform the thankless tasks of mothering with her youngest that forged their bond, and which compelled her fiery-tongued, but faithful *mangnae* to think of her and care for her in a way that her older children did not. But this was all much later. For now, Sa Mi spent her days waking up to the fading summer air, interrupted by hearkening ribbons of cool breezes from the North that apparently only she could feel. The turn of the atmosphere magnified her loneliness and awoke a talent she never knew she possessed, but that endeared her even more to her doting father-in-law. While everyone was stunted by the humidity still blanketing that land of rugged mountains in late August, she announced one day to her father-in-law:

"The harvest will come early this year *aboneem*, autumn will elude us. We must save the crop before the winter frost catches us by surprise."

The old man stared at his young daughter-in-law, dumbfounded by her premonition as the beads of sweat behind his ears belied her very words. Still, as he had learned from his dead wife on several occasions, one could not contend with the sharp, deadly precision of a woman's intuition. Too often he could not hide his shock when his wife would ask him almost word for word about the very thoughts that ran through his mind regarding the significant yet mundane casualties of daily life that he had rationalized would remain better concealed to save them both time and the wastefulness of words.

He never made the mistake to challenge his wife when she felt inspired to read back the transcript generating in his mind. In this way they shared a very peaceful life together, unlike many of his peers who thought it their right to withhold the truth from their wives. When his wife was seized abruptly by a violent fever that left no time for a proper goodbye or all the words he had failed to share with her, he was at least relieved that he wasn't one of those men whose tempers frightened their wives into submission, that is, whatever relief he could feel during those dark days of grief.

The patriarch decided he would concede to the lesson he learned throughout his marriage and from his deceased wife. He also considered that his daughter-in-law's pregnancy helped compound her mysterious female faculties for prophecy.

"Is that so?" he finally replied nodding his head.

As Sa Mi bowed her head, the servants who had overheard the exchange could not believe their ears. It was hard enough for them to keep up with their chores in the oppressive heat, but to prepare for an early harvest underneath an unforgiving August sun? Not even one of the field hands who had worked the land year after year and rose and labored to the rhythms of the earth, could confirm Sa Mi's prediction. In fact, they were quite reluctant to do so.

Sa Mi had even surprised herself with her prediction. It seemed as if the words just leapt out of her mouth before she could even decode them herself. But once they were spoken, she knew with absolute certainty that her intuition was correct. She simply surmised that this new-found faculty was another sign of her stepping into the reins of womanhood, just like her impending motherhood was another such sign.

Sa Mi's newly-acquired perception toward the rhythms of the atmosphere only aggravated her lonely state and tricked her into a sadness that was really not her right to bear. After all, unlike some newly-minted daughters-in-law, she did not suffer from the abuses of a jealous mother-in-law (though she did find her step mother-in-law to be aloof and distant). She was endowed with that God-given gift of fertility. She loved her husband and he returned her love with a reserved quietude. *And* her father-in-law adored her. She was indeed considered to be a fortunate woman for her time. *Still*, she thought to herself, *such experiences lose their capacity for joy when your mother is not there to share it with you.*

So it was in this state that Sa Mi eagerly anticipated the weekly arrival of the old sesame seed oil peddler.

"Chan kirum!" Sa Mi heard the familiar voice that had over the years become like background noise. Every day was like a rotating market parade of peddlers: the cabbage lady boasting the largest and freshest *pe-chu* perfect for the *kimchi* that Sa Mi had become an expert at fermenting; the ginseng peddler who always came promptly after lunchtime every week with an arrogance about the powerful medicinal properties of his rare batch found only on an isolated mountain near a virgin stream; and the sly fish peddler who often added a few more grams to the weight of the fish if one wasn't paying attention. Everything else was either grown on the estate or painstakingly handmade by Sa Mi herself with the help of the servants. With her husband's fertile holdings, they were never, at least in those days, in want of that heaven of every meal: rice.

"Chan kirum!"

Sesame seed oil however, was one delicacy that they often purchased from the peddler as it was more fruitful to do so than to spend the arduous hours trying to extract the tasty oil from the tiny sesame seeds, which aromatic and rich essence was used as a seasoning to flavor almost everything.

Something compelled Sa Mi to look up that day from her search for her hairpin when she saw the old lady hunched over from the weight of the bottles of oil on her back. She immediately thought of her own mother carrying her loads of *pe-chu* every day to the market after her husband died so that Sa Mi could go to school. Sa Mi dropped what she was doing to run to the gate.

"Ajumma!" she called to the older woman, bowing her head, "won't you come in for a moment? We have just finished our last drop of oil."

The sun-cracked, wrinkled face looked up to see the young lady of the house addressing her and bowed her head, "Good morning my lady, very nice to see you." Honest to the core she continued, "I would love to sell to you again, but you must not have heard that I just sold to one of your helpers yesterday. Surely you have not already gone through all of those bottles?"

"Yes, of course, "Sa Mi replied, "But you can never have enough sesame oil in the house, please, come in."

Sa Mi led her inside the courtyard and asked her to take a seat, indicating to one of the servants to bring some cold barley tea for the *chankirum ajumma*.

As the old lady got settled and released the heavy bag from her back, she let out a sigh of relief, "My goodness, summer is unforgiving this year! Thank you, my lady, for allowing me to rest with you," then squinting her eyes now that she was close up and could see Sa Mi's flawless beauty, "My, what a beautiful face!"

As was often the case when someone acknowledged Sa Mi's beauty – her complexion like a lotus blossom in a clear, crystal lake – heat began to form on her cheeks and she bowed her head in embarrassment.

"Made all the more beautiful by the glow of motherhood," the kind woman added.

Sa Mi, who was not yet showing, especially through the modest *hanbok* she wore that matted any obvious curves, looked up in surprise, but the wrinkled face simply smiled back. Sa Mi discerned that the old woman shared her new-found telepathy but applied it to individuals and not to the atmosphere.

"Perhaps I can one day find a nice daughter-in-law like you for my son."

As a servant placed two glasses of refreshing tea before the two women Sa Mi replied, "You have a son?" wondering if she too, like her own mother had done years before, was struggling to send her son to school.

"Oh, yes, little Suk-won. He will turn sixteen this fall. He is actually on the other side of town peddling the rest of the oil. We cover more area this way."

"Oh, so he's not at school right now?"

Looking slightly ashamed the old lady replied, "No, I am afraid he's not, he does not even remember his father's face."

Sa Mi felt embarrassed for saying anything as it was clear that the young boy had been working ever since he was able in order to help feed them.

"It is a shame because he is such a smart boy," she continued, "He created a machine to crush the sesame seeds just so the oil could be extracted for sale," grinning to herself, "For as long as I can remember, he always loved building things, taking them apart then putting them back together, it is a talent you know."

"Yes," Sa Mi nodded her head respectfully, "and the oil is so delicious." It was indeed one of the finest she had tasted which is why she ceased buying the oil from the market peddlers but relied on the old lady's visits. "Where do you get your sesame seeds?"

"We grow our own," then chuckling, "you can imagine how many seeds it must take to make just one bottle of oil so the rest we buy since we don't have the land to grow more and my son picks through all the seeds for only the very best ones. I've never seen a child work like him," her eyes dimming in sadness, "he is very determined. He says that someday we will have acres of our own land with only the best quality sesame seeds and that by then he will have developed an even better machine to squeeze the oil from the seed. Maybe by then he will also have met a nice, young lady like yourself to take care of him," she said, winking at Sa Mi.

Throughout her moments of conversation with the old lady, Sa Mi's loneliness started to break up into indecipherable pieces, and she cursed herself the days she spent feeling sorry for herself.

"You must be so proud of him," Sa Mi replied, wondering if her own mother ever spoke about her to strangers, beaming as the woman before her glowed with love.

"I am. I just wish I had more to offer him. Do you know that I had the idea to write our names and 'sesame oil' on these bottles, just for fun you know, to make it look pretty, but that I never learned my letters? And I have also deprived my own child from learning his letters, and now I cannot even teach him!"

Without hesitation Sa Mi declared, "I could teach you!"

The old lady's eyes rounded and her eyebrows jumped up, "I am far too old!" she replied.

"No, no you can learn, I know you can. I'm very patient, and well, it would mean so much to me to be able to do this. You have to come this way anyway, right? We could spend an hour a day. That won't take too much time away from you, will it? And you can then teach your son!"

"But what have I to offer you for your time and generosity?" Looking through her sack she pulled out a canvas bag filled to the top, "this is the residue left over from the seeds after the oil has been extracted. It makes excellent livestock feed, but we haven't any livestock to feed, and I doubt I can get very much for it...as you can see there is not much of it, but I hate to see it go to waste. Please take it; it is the only way that I can accept your generous offer."

"*Ajumma* I want you to know that it would be a blessing for me to be able to teach you, but if you insist on my accepting this wonderful feed, I graciously accept," bowing her head and accepting the bag with both hands.

"Very well then," the old lady responded getting up and smiling. "We have a deal. I will bring you the protein residue from the sesame seeds in exchange for my lessons. Are you sure you can teach an old lady like myself?"

"Positive," responded Sa Mi, elated for the first time in months to be exercising her erudition once again.

"All right then, let us start next week around this time?"

"That will be wonderful, oh, but wait, please," said Sa Mi starting at the sight of the woman placing the heavy sack on her back. "I would like to purchase the rest of your oil, except of course, the ones you have reserved for others."

"Are you sure?" the kind peddler asked with a hint of skepticism.

"Yes. I think they are delicious and I would like to give them away to our friends. May I?" Sa Mi asked, reaching into her coin purse dangling from her sash.

"Yes, yes of course, let me just pull two each for Mrs. Kim and Mrs. Park as they both are due today for an order. The rest are yours. Thank you very much."

After the business transaction took place and Sa Mi bid her guest farewell, Sa Mi returned to the search for her hairpin – now with a lighter step. Excited about her new friendship, she thought about how the words of one person could lift you through your moments of solitude. Indeed, these were words that had been touched by the wisdom of the saintly widow who did not skip one day of work throughout her gritty existence.

Sa Mi looked forward to the lessons with the sesame oil peddler like a beaming light at the end of a long tunnel. Though she adored her husband with the subdued affection that one worships their Creator, silently and seriously, their time away from each other during the day left her to her own devices. She kept busy those days supervising the preparations for the harvest and the care of her stepdaughter whose fussiness over the injustice of her fate continued with full force. But throughout the days, it was hard to stave off the pangs of loneliness that took her by surprise.

Sa Mi's secret lessons with the old woman quickly went from once a week, to twice a week, to every lunch hour. In this way, Sa Mi began teaching the widow the script of Japanese which was the official language after the annexation, as well as *hangul*, or the Korean script that the Japanese sought to eradicate. The old widow possessed an aptitude for learning and soon wielded the pen as if she had known how to use it since birth. Throughout those hour lessons, when she was practicing the tidy strokes of *hangul* the student would entertain her teacher with stories of her travels and the more personal secrets of the homes in the neighborhood.

"There is a shaman that occupies the house down the way."

Sa Mi knew right away to which house and family she was referring, everyone knew about the mysterious youngest daughter from the prosperous household who spoke in trembles with her hands. But Sa Mi was not one to gossip and she quickly changed the subject to escape her uneasiness and her superstition that spreading words of the misfortunes of others might provoke such calamity to befall her own home.

But the old lady continued, noting Sa Mi's discomfort, but compelled to get her thoughts out.

"Her parents ignore her. Pretend she doesn't exist. They keep her hidden from view. Imagine being shunned in such a manner by your own family. What will the poor girl do? I worry about her. I sense tragedy on the horizon."

"It must be very difficult for her parents, her family to cope. I understand the young woman does not speak, and erupts in terrible outbursts," responded Sa Mi cautiously.

"This is true. It is a parents' job to love. Seems so effortless, and yet, in practice, so complicated."

"Yes," Sa Mi added, bowing her head, "my sister believes my parents were too idealistic in rearing us, so that she finds herself unhappy in her married life, as the constant loving support didn't prepare her for the difficulties of the future," Sa Mi reflected on her beloved Heebin, who she hadn't spoken to in months.

"Hmm," sighed ajumma, "I suppose these are all issues you must ponder, eh?" she winked, referring to the growing life in Sa Mi's belly. "Still, it seems, that love, and love alone, is what provides the pillar of strength to confront life head-on."

Sa Mi paused and looked up. She had felt so barren and lost when her parents died, and even now, speaking to the old sesame oil peddler, she felt a longing for them as the same permanence of death descended upon her, "My mother said the same thing when my father died. That the only certainty in life is love and love alone."

"Yes," the old woman whispered, her eyes glassing over, "indeed, love, and love alone," she nodded.

Feeling the presence of her own mother through the old sesame seed oil peddler's gaze, Sa Mi breathed in deeply.

As the days passed by in this manner, Sa Mi sought to keep all her bubbling thoughts at bay in light of the fact that her days with the old sesame seed oil peddler were numbered. Sa Mi had made tremendous progress with her new friend and had opened up a whole new world to her.

Though Sa Mi seldom saw the kind widow in the years to come, as life often interfered and seized both of them into its labors, she thought of her during each and every one of her following seven pregnancies, always recalling the terror of the first, and conquering the fear of each subsequent one until the loneliness of her earlier years had transitioned into wisdom. This wasn't of course, until many years later. And just as the widow had surmised, Sa Mi found motherhood, and the seemingly simple charge of loving one's child, deeply vexing.

The Least Loved

By the time Sa Mi's sister-in-law gave birth to a boy, Sa Mi had given birth for the second time as well and the house was bubbling over with the chaos of children.

Soonjin, the oldest, no longer cried but wore an expression of impudence, her longing for her birth mother replaced by a steel casing over her heart though she was barely six years old. It would be her first year at school and while there were plenty of attendants to help her prepare for it, her natural self-possession, and perhaps the void inside of her, propelled an independence that put everyone at arm's length. She meticulously dressed herself, combed her own hair, and was ready to leave for that unknown journey outside of the house without a trace of fear on her scowled demeanor. Soon never revealed her jealousy toward her new siblings who occupied all of her stepmother's time. It was not that she was deprived of any *more* attention now that her brother and sister were born, she had gotten used to that unexplainable feeling inside of her that convinced her she would never quite belong. In fact, her disappointment toward the adults around her exceeded any ill feeling she had toward her siblings. Her father had a way of revealing an expression of pure joy with the two siblings that was matched only by a shadow of guilt and a look of pity when he turned his attentions toward her. As soon as the opportunity became available, she was ready to see what the rest of the world had to offer her.

Sa Mi soon discovered that she was not made for the nurturing role of domestic life. Fortunately, her social status saved her from changing the dirty diapers and attending to all of the day-to-day exhaustions that constituted motherhood. Even with these advantages, she was still worn out from nursing her baby girl (who she gladly handed over to a nursemaid when the finicky child would allow) and chasing after the girl's toddler brother whose curiosity was insatiable. Consumed as she was by the bedlam two children bring into a household, she could barely recall that she had felt so all alone with the ghosts just years earlier and was unmoved when her sister-in-law burst through the front door. The catty woman donned a Western hat on her head and held her bundle of joy as a badge of honor as she traipsed into Sa Mi's home.

"I was wondering when you were going to come visit me to extend your congratulations!" the sister-in-law blurted.

"*Hyeongnim*," Sa Mi started, and then looking down at the baby suckling at her breast, "I have been quite busy myself," the staunch conviction of motherhood had replaced Sa Mi's timid nature. She did not bother to remind Sowae that she had visited their home several times since the baby boy had been born.

"Oh yes, but having a boy is so special!" Sowae replied.

Realizing that motherhood had not changed her sister-in-law at all, Sa Mi ignored her, "And my niece, where is she?" Sa Mi asked, looking around for a toddler her son's age.

"She's at home," the distracted woman responded, still not looking up, then thrusting the bundle under Sa Mi's nose, "Just look at him, doesn't he look like an angel? I think he looks just like his *haraboji*, oh and how father adores him."

"Yes he is," Sa Mi nodded, "he is beautiful."

After bantering on and on like this for several minutes and without obtaining the full reception she had hoped for, Sowae started, "Well, I must get going, he is quite popular and everyone is dying to meet him you know. I'll come by again soon." She then walked out of the door as if it had been any other day, not once asking Sa Mi about her own children, not even to ridicule her about the oldest who was not her own.

It was during these years that Sa Mi was jolted into womanhood and any illusions she still harbored about continuing her education or teaching others like she had the sesame seed oil peddler, diminished. She was now terrorized by the unending needs of children. Every two to three years for the next *eighteen* years another Yi child would enter the world consuming Sa Mi's mind and body.

At the time however, Sa Mi could not predict any of the events that were to follow, other than the senses of the wind and sky and the palpability of the earth which continued to win her favor among her husband and father-in-law. She simply lacked the time to reflect on much during that tenuous era, and those that did ponder the fate of the country were bewildered by what would become of their tiny nation. There were opinions abound on how to move forward and plenty of disagreement.

Many openly opposed the occupation and fled into exile to bring the country's plight before the international stage. Some insisted that armed struggle was the only way to defeat their oppressive tyrant, and still others extolled the virtues of modernization and the superiority of the colonizers.

On the other end of the opposition struggle a movement was brewing that insisted not only on liberation, but a complete social revolution to overthrow the existing structure of society.

Among these various viewpoints was a longing that hung from the shoulders of ordinary people. It was a longing for a better future, one that remembered the nostalgia of the past and lived through the suffering of the present.

It was a restless longing, a gnawing uncertainty about the meaning of the subtle gestures and outright violence of the occupation. It was Sun's draining dignity of having to answer to Japanese officials regarding the ownership of the land that had belonged to his family for generations. It was the disappearing Korean classics in the schools. It was the imposition of Japanese names to replace the storied histories of their family surnames. It was the sidelong glances at Sa Mi by the military police as she walked through the village square. It was holding your posture upright and wearing the legacy of your ancestors in the face of humiliation. Sa Mi and her family were among the lives suffocating under the weight of this longing, and their testament here is proof that they had ever lived.

As the children grew older and multiplied in number, her sister-in-law's visits to Sa Mi resumed and became more frequent. Though Sa Mi had to tolerate Sowae's envy and off-handed remarks, the visits offered both of them a brief interlude from their domestic lives and the tense boredom of the occupation. Their children, a growing arsenal of cousins, would entertain one another and the sisters-in-law grew closer by virtue of their shared struggles as wives and mothers. Sowae still maintained her competitive spirit however, and never let a moment pass where she saw fit to remind Sa Mi of her inferiority.

Even though dusk started to close-in, the children merrily continued their game of marbles and socialized in the courtyard by the light of the full moon. They would continue like this until they heard their father's footsteps encroaching toward the house and then they would scatter. Nobody was interested in being the subject of Sun's wrath though they all – except for Soonjin – endured it to varying degrees.

Soonjin, who received only her father's pity and guilt, and not much of anything from her stepmother Sa Mi, sat in the courtyard with a book enveloped within another book. Though she would have preferred some privacy away from her other siblings, none of the children wanted to be inside the house and near Sa Mi who was undergoing her most recent turmoil, a fifth pregnancy, which she made no secrets of her attempts to terminate.

In the absence of their parents, Soonjin commanded a respect from her siblings that she dutifully reinforced at every opportunity. "Hey! Keep it down," she warned from behind her book to the two youngest boys who had erupted into a tussle over their game of marbles.

Jongjin, the older by eleven months was gifted with an incisive mind and often ran circles around his younger brother, Eujin, who he effortlessly dominated in every aspect of life, apparently including marbles. Eujin often erupted in tears of frustration, his sensitive soul capable of bearing only so much from his talented older brother.

"Bongjin-ya!" Soonjin called out to her stepmother's first-born and most-treasured. The handsome boy was sitting with his sister Mijin and cousin Yeonjin, and promptly stood up after hearing his name barked out by his older sister. Only his father and older sister called out his name with such an air of contempt, and they repeatedly called his name to issue blame for one offense or another, all throughout the day, every day. This time the offense – as indicated with a nod of Soonjin's head - was the altercation between the two brothers which was apparently Bongjin's responsibility to officiate.

Having grown used to, but never understanding his sister's disdain for him and her cold detachment generally, Bongjin went over to comfort Eujin, and pulled aside Jongjin.

"You have to let him win every now and then," Bongjin instructed, "Look at him, he can't grow up always thinking that he is inferior, that's not good for him."

Jongjin, the only son that received praise from his father, unlike the abuses Sun doled out to Bongjin, eyed his older brother skeptically, "You want me to let him win? On purpose?"

"Yes, not all the time. Every now and then. Let him feel the glory of winning too."

Jongjin, whose entitlement reigned supreme, and who even looked down on his oldest brother despite Confucian dictates, simply replied, "I disagree with your methods and logic, but I'll consider it."

Such disrespect to an elder brother would normally not be tolerated, but the generous-hearted Bongjin let it slide, "Disagree if you like, but show him some kindness."

Jongjin pondered this. Kindness was not something that his father rewarded. In fact, it was Bongjin's kindness that seemed to irritate their father more than anything as of late.

Soonjin looked up from her book which introduced concepts like the class struggle and the suffering of the masses. The content appeared to be beyond her pubescent head and she seemed to have acquired it through dubious means, given that her father could be immediately jailed and killed for possessing communist literature. The taboo nature of the content had interested her and reading it in plain view under her father's roof evoked a titillating satisfaction within her.

Observing Bongjin Soonjin let out a sigh. There was a kinship she felt with her father due to their mutual disdain for her brother which she also found satisfying. The resentment she felt for her father ran parallel to her desire to identify with him and to occupy a place in his heart. Though Sun had celebrated and toasted Bongjin's birth with fanfare, once Bongjin arrived and his personality began to form, Sun was quite cruel to his first-born. Soonjin appreciated the mistreatment Bongjin received and freely joined in to remind him of his shortcomings.

Her sister Mijin however, was a different story. Soonjin watched her sitting side-by-side with her beloved cousin Yeonjin. Mijin escaped the fierce and burning jealousy conferred onto her by her sister, by seeking sisterhood from her cousin instead. The cousins became quite close as a result.

Soonjin didn't identify the deep loathing in the pit of her stomach for her sister as jealousy, instead she insisted that she simply had nothing in common with the empty-headed and shallow human being who was her father's only legitimate daughter. That Sun saved all his affections for Mijin, having only pity for Soon, contempt for Bongjin, and cool indifference for the younger boys, was not lost on Soonjin. Sa Mi who could barely maintain eye contact with Soonjin, lit up at the sight of her only daughter.

Soonjin thought, as she often did when observing the two girls, that they were an odd pair. And she actually didn't mind her cousin Yeonjin, who suffered such gross mistreatment by her repulsive mother. Sowae, Sa Mi's sister-in-law, never minded to acknowledge her daughter's existence which is why Yeon was always at their home.

When the two cousins were together it never seemed that Yeon said much of anything, it was always Mijin droning on about the colors of her dress, her favorite dolls, or the foods she liked to eat. Her cousin Yeon was her quiet audience. Such is the nature of entitlement, Soonjin came to understand. To be most-loved like Mijin and Jongjin was to stake a place in your world, assert your desires, and carry on about them as if everyone else depended on your opinions. The dynamic seemed to be self-reinforcing, as the more the most-loved ones behaved in this manner the more praise they seemed to receive.

The least-loved ones like her cousin Yeon however, often just listened and said very little. And no matter how many talents and virtues Yeon exhibited – as she was intelligent, beautiful, graceful, and certainly more interesting than Mijin – the more she was shut down by her parents and dismissed.

Though Soonjin knew she was least-loved, she decided early on that she would not wear the look of defeat. She derided it in her brother when she witnessed the pained look on his sensitive face after a lashing from their father. And while she liked her cousin Yeon, Soonjin despised the way Yeon endured such humiliation from her mother. It was evident the mistreatment was chipping away at her soul. Soonjin on the other hand promised herself to never show such vulnerability. Ever. Nobody would ever be able to get to her. She would be sure of that.

Soonjin continued to read about armed struggle and putting forth a resistance. And while she didn't fully understand all the intricacies of capitalist economies and the oppression of the masses, something about the material resonated with her.

As she heard the steady footsteps of her father outside the gate, she put her finger to her lips to shush her siblings. When they too heard that it was indeed their father approaching, they all picked up their items and scattered.

Nobody wanted to be subject to Sun's wrath, especially as of late.

Sun Meets an Old Friend

Yi Sun Soo was seated at the local *tabang*, nursing a cup of tea as he waited for his friend. He was not his usual outgoing self but reverted into the gloomy outfit he assumed after experiencing a string of gambling losses. Now that his father had passed, he had full ownership of the smaller portion of land that was passed onto him, his father's more substantial holdings having been relegated to his older brother under the dictates of family law.

Ever since his father's death a few years ago, Sun sensed a foreboding that he dismissed as the grief that inevitably strikes after one has lost a parent. He now had five children at home and his hold on his remaining estate slackened as the Japanese tightened their grip and threatened to appropriate some of his holdings. The source of this grip could be traced to the new Governor General who generated a tide of uneasiness among the people and whose wrath had already been felt by the likes of Sun. The Japanese officials were particularly hostile in his part of the country as it was known to be bubbling with subversive activity. Though Sun and his father had themselves not been implicated in any nationalistic activity, and often tried to appease the government by offering extra rations of grain for the military, it seemed that the more compliant they were, the greedier the Japanese became. And whenever they were suspicious of any of Sun's tenants, which they often were, he was paid a visit by the local officials and told that as landlord he needed to keep better watch of his tenants. It had been a tense few years for Sun and his restlessness did not serve him well.

On this particular day, Sun's anxiety was palpable as he waited for a childhood friend who was now a journalist for the Gwangju-ilbo newspaper. The paper was on the brink of being shut down by the government for seditious activity and it was a risky venture to meet with Childong for he had been tagged by the authorities. Sun planned to meet him at the *tabang* during noon on Monday, knowing that it was not frequented at that hour, and hoping to limit the opportunities for Japanese police disguised as civilians to harass them. He picked a table that was far away from anyone else and acknowledged customers in the tea house as they extended their deferential greetings to him.

The old friends would be careful of how they talked and would address each other by the names the Japanese had forced upon them. Despite the risks, Sun always took the opportunity to meet with Childong because they shared fond memories from their childhood. As young boys they could often be found running around the estate while their fathers, who were also friends from the days before the Japanese, met every now and then to share a few bottles of soju and memories. Childong's father had died suddenly of a heart attack when Childong was barely thirteen and with three older sisters who had no claim to the land, and few other relatives, it was easy for the Japanese to come and appropriate most of his family's holdings, leaving Childong with virtually nothing. Sun's father had tried to intervene during those times, but there was nothing he could do as he was not family and had no legal rights in the matter. Instead, Sun's father did the best he could for the orphaned boy, putting Childong through school with his own sons.

Childong dealt with his plight by blaming everything bad that happened to him on the Japanese. His circumstances fueled a determination in him that compelled him to excel in his studies while Sun indulged in his leisurely activities, composing his poetic verses when the spirit moved him. The years of school had only made the budding journalist angrier as he witnessed his professors carted away for subversive activity and seen the Korean classics on which he had been reared, disappear from the curriculum and be replaced with stories of the glory of the Japanese empire. Childong vowed within the circle of artists, writers, and students with whom he associated that he would see justice one day in his lifetime, and that as a journalist, he would reveal the truth of the occupation to the world one way or other.

Sun admired his friend for his convictions, beliefs that Sun sometimes channeled through his pages of poetry, but Childong had given up asking his friend to join him at some of the underground meetings he faithfully attended with other political allies. Sun recalled his friend's final plea a couple years ago with great clarity.

"This is the last time I'm going to ask you to attend one of our meetings. You must understand that this is the only way we will be able to topple our oppressors. Give up that gambling habit of yours that the oppressors have manipulated you into exercising. Don't you see that all the money you lose eventually goes into *their* mouths to feed *their* military and to pay for the bullets that have *our* names on them? I know you do it to escape your sorrow, but there's something else you can do, something for your country, something for your people."

It was times like these that irritated Sun, when his friend would start in with his nationalist fervor he sounded like a man possessed. To even suggest that Sun's gambling habit was somehow indirectly supporting the Japanese occupation was, in Sun's mind, absurd. Yet Sun continued to meet with his childhood friend just to experience the relief of seeing Childong alive. Sun didn't know for how long he would see him that way and seeing him in the flesh provided him with a comfort that perhaps things were not as bad as they seemed. Whenever Childong would start in with one of his diatribes, Sun wanted to ask him, "What good are you to your country and your family after the Japanese have thrown you in jail, shipped you off to one of its labor camps, or even worse, killed you?"

If Sun were ever to entertain the idea of getting involved with Childong's group of dissenters, he would never hear the end of it from his wife who begged and pleaded with him to stay away from his friend's gatherings and any other activity that would arouse suspicion from the Japanese. She did not ask much of him, and this was one request that Sun would honor.

However, Sun did continue to exercise the caution to meet with Childong alone, not only as a caring old friend, but as a concerned citizen who was hungry for the truth of what was going on in the rest of the country and in the world, and not the sing-song propaganda that the Japanese fed them through the mainstream papers. To Sun, the truth in and of itself was empowering, what he chose to do with it should and would come later, he surmised. He was too cautious a character to jump blindly into any decisions without thinking them through thoroughly. The one area in his life that betrayed his own instincts was his gambling. Sun's sound reason was contrary to the thrill of the game which belonged to the purview of luck and fortune. Unfortunately, luck and fortune did not often favor him at the gambling table, and yet, he felt it was the only place where he could exercise his freedom, the only place where his steadfast reason did not intervene.

Sun picked up his pen and his chapbook, recalling that his friend was habitually late, and began to write the first line of a poem: *Where with sunset fortune roams, in the mind set freedom moans...*

Just then he felt a hand on his shoulder and someone say, "When are you going to let me start publishing some of those?"

Sun turned around to the familiar voice of his childhood friend wearing his signature mischievous smile.

Without drawing attention to themselves they exchanged affectionate greetings and sat down when Sun raised his eyebrow at Childong's affected appearance. He had a fading black eye and a line running down his left cheek.

Leaning in Childong whispered, "It's all just part of the job."

They had mastered a way of communicating with each other where a third party would be lost of the main stream of conversation. Within the first five minutes Sun learned that his friend had been roughed up by the police and taken in. He had been released just one week earlier after being "caught" in public with a group of more than four.

"It was actually only three of us walking, but none of us are much favored by them. We're not meeting anymore like we used to. We must find other ways."

The two immediately began catching up on the course of their lives. Sun informed Childong of the number of children he had so far, and Childong recounted his latest love affair. Unlike Sun he was not married but seemed to have a different girlfriend every time they met. Sun thought that Childong's single lifestyle further justified the foolhardy risks he took which prevented him from thinking more long-term, more responsibly, more with an eye toward self-preservation. In his defense, Childong argued that he did not need a woman interfering with his more important focus of liberation.

After the personal topics were covered, the two friends lowered their voices and Childong talked about what he knew about the country's state of affairs. They jumped from topic to topic and in their characteristic way proceeded in their disjointed conversation:

"It's continuing with full force." *There was no end in sight to the rightist military movement in Japan.*

"And the invasion?" Sun replied.

"It appears they will take Beijing."

Sun leaned back in his chair after hearing the news. Japan's campaign to invade all of China was off to a successful start. If Beijing were to fall, Shanghai and Nanking were not far behind. Sun realized what was at the root of his foreboding earlier as he was waiting for his friend.

Seeing the discouragement on his friend's face, the journalist continued, "You know, they're increasing the raids."

The raids on individual homes. Military men were known to raid homes in the middle of the night to gather Koreans to be shipped off to fight the war in China or work in its labor camps in Manchuokuo.[1] Sun neither needed to prompt his friend on the progress of the invasion, nor the threat of the raids as it was clear that without the intervention of the US or Britain, there were no limits to Japan's power. He also knew that given his friend's background, Childong's sisters' families were probably on a list somewhere to be raided and shipped away. The Japanese knew that the easiest way to get to you was by getting to your family first. Sun correctly surmised that the only reason Childong had gotten out of jail this time was because his brother-in-law, an important businessman, was very friendly with some influential Japanese. Needless to say, this pro-Japanese businessman was not fond of Childong.

---

[1] Manchuria.

Just then an unfamiliar man entered the *tabang* and Sun, who had the better angle, quickly gave the signal to his friend. They switched topics.

"So how about the Olympics?" Sun asked, as the stranger eyed them suspiciously before taking a seat at the table next to the two men. Sun knew everybody in these surrounding areas and given his brother's political role, everybody knew who he was. It was clear to Sun that this man was not an innocent passer-by.

"Everyone is eagerly anticipating the marathon race," Childong replied, trying to cover his bruised face.

Sun cursed himself for bringing up the Olympics at all, knowing his friend would provide such an unpatriotic answer. In his response, Childong was referring to Son Ki-Jong, the Korean marathon runner who was running for the Japanese in the Olympics as all the Korean Olympic athletes in 1936 were. Any victories by these athletes would be claimed by Japan. What they were talking about could be construed as nationalistic. After the waitress placed a cup of tea before the stranger, he stood up and walked toward the two men.

Holding up his identification and declaring that he had been sent by the Office of the Governor General, he asked the two men to identify themselves. He did this knowing full well who they were as he had clearly followed Childong to the *tabang*. Asking them to identify themselves was just another form of humiliation, as they were expected to answer using their Japanese names or risk being taken in.

Sun, concerned about the fate of his friend, answered first, "Kaneda Tei." His friend continued to sit, his hand still covering the side of his bruised face.

The military man took this as insolence and repeated his order with added vehemence. "State your name under the demands of the empire's governor-general!" By this time the *tabang* owners and the few people in the tea house were all looking on at the commotion. Sun noticed uniformed policemen walk by the entrance, oblivious to what looked like just another event in the lives of the occupation.

Childong continued to stare down at the table. Sun looked at his friend wide-eyed, wondering what was going through his mind. Finally, the lanky body unfolded from the chair, and stood up straight to face the policeman square in the eye - yet another display of insolence. Sun wondered if his friend was on a suicide mission for the both of them.

In a deadpan voice the bold journalist answered his interrogator in Korean:

"Choi Childong."

This elicited a smirk from the officer who gritted his teeth and spat out in Japanese, "We don't recognize your dirty Korean *josaeng-jin!*" and he followed with a forceful punch to the abdomen that caused the journalist to lose his breath. At that moment, the two officers who had walked by earlier entered the *tabang* to apprehend Childong. Sun quickly began to talk to the officer in his perfect Japanese.

"Please, there must be some mistake. I am the landlord of this area and this man has done nothing wrong. You can check with our local office. Our land has supported the Japanese military with our grain and we were simply meeting over tea as old friends." Sun glanced over the man's face to see if he would take a bribe, but then realized his own pockets were empty from his earlier gambling slew.

"This man is wanted for treason, a crime punishable by death. I have the good mind to take you in as well for conspiring with an enemy of the empire."

Childong regained his composure and stated, "This man supports your beloved empire and he is no more than a Japanese-loving sycophant! It's me you want. Don't waste your time with him. He has friends in the governor-general's office that you will not want to contend with if you make the mistake of laying a finger on him. And just so you know, I have already served my time and was promptly released…"

"You shut up!" The Japanese officer spat out, "You were wrongfully released and will be held indefinitely for treason and acting as an enemy of the empire!" He landed another blow to the stomach as the other two officers held onto either side. He then glanced at Sun who indeed looked well-connected and decided not to risk ruffling his feathers in case what the lanky Korean had said was true. The officer's mission was to go after the journalist and his impertinent friends, he had not bargained on running into this landlord.

"Dirty Koreans," he muttered, then looking back at his captive, "your friend is lucky this time." They then walked out as Sun watched them go in disbelief. He assured the others in the *tabang* not to worry and to proceed with their business, that it had all been a terrible mistake, and apologized to the owners for the disruption.

After stopping at home to get more money and waving away his wife's inquiries into his preoccupied demeanor, he headed for the local council office to see the head chief, who over the years had accepted several bribes from Sun to keep away from his estate.

The meeting however, proved fruitless. "I'm sorry Mr. Tei, this was a directive from the governor-general's office in Gyeongseong and I have no power over them. Your friend is in deep trouble, you should consider yourself fortunate for not having been mixed up in all of this," he answered, raising his eyebrow as a matter of rebuke. He then held out the palm of his hand, "It is of course, always a pleasure to be paid a visit by you, and I will be sure to let the officer involved know that he could have conducted his matters with a little more respect."

Sun laid the customary "tip" in the officer's hand, his pride bubbling over in his chest, and then went on his way. For security reasons they would not allow him to see his friend at the jail but told him he could return the following afternoon.

Sun laid awake all night re-playing the events of the day and wondered if he could have paid-off the officers on the spot had he not gambled away all of his cash earlier. He cursed his friend for not following his lead, but instead, begged for more humiliation by acting out the way he did. Sun wondered how he would bail Childong out of jail this time and kept his mind from drifting to all the torturous tactics they must be using on him to get a confession. It made him sick to his stomach. Sun also kept himself from thoughts that he might not ever see his friend again.

The next morning a servant rushed toward him with the edition of the same newspaper that Childong wrote for. The big news was two-fold. First, the heroic Korean marathon runner had won the gold medal across the globe in Berlin and was featured on the front page with his medal. But the real news required an even closer look. One could see that the photograph was touched up so that the rising sun on the athlete's jersey, which symbolized the empire of Japan, was noticeably smudged out. Some brave editor at the paper saw fit to publicly besmirch the oppressor. Koreans both celebrated and mourned in private. This would be the end of the paper.

That afternoon Sun promptly made his way back to the jail to inquire about his friend. The officers pleaded ignorance and insisted that no one by that name had been brought in. Desperate and exhausted, Sun reminded them about their conversation just a day earlier, but they replied that they did not know what he was talking about. One young desk clerk wore the pained expression of guilt so Sun pulled him aside to talk to him. He looked scared and shameful. Though Sun didn't recognize him, the young man had been the recipient of many of the landlord's generosities and couldn't bear carrying on the charade.

"You know what happened to my friend, young man. I can see you know something, you must tell me as this has all been a very terrible mistake."

"Sir," the young man whispered, looking up as his voice shook, "if my chief finds out I told…"

"He won't, I will not betray you, but you must tell me where he is."

"To be honest, I don't know," he stammered, "that is the truth, he is not here. They transported him…"

"Where? Where did they take him?"

"I don't know, all I know is…"

"Yes?"

"He was unconscious, and they took him away."

Someone walked by as he said this so Sun released his hold on the young man and thanked him for his help. It was clear that he really didn't know where Childong had been taken. Sun then went back to the local chief's office to hear more of the same claims of ignorance.

"It is not my purview. There's no way of me knowing what happened to your friend. It is of course, always a pleasure…"

When Sun finally returned home, defeated and drained, he had the sinking feeling that the government had smudged out any trace of his childhood friend, just as the Gwangju-ilbo newspaper had sought to smudge out the rising empire.

Closing in on Hunger and Desire

On December 8, 1941, the country was in a celebratory mood. All the mainstream newspapers displayed front-page headlines of the Imperial Nation's successful attack on Pearl Harbor and America's humiliating defeat. The attack sealed Japan's plans to sweep through Southeast Asia and expand her empire through Burma, Malaya, the East Indies and the Philippines. The Japanese had already advanced their aggression into China, and the victory in Pearl Harbor would encourage them to exploit the countries in the Pacific for much needed fuel and resources. They had already exhausted and squeezed every last drop out of their colony of Korea.

Citizens stood in line in front of Shinto shrines to pray for Japan's victory in the war and a renewed vigor was felt all along the Korean peninsula as a decree was announced that every act should be made in support of the war effort.

Sa Mi did not share in the celebratory spirit. She sat nursing her sixth child who she had carried with great difficulty and with whom she had experienced equal trials with during the labor. She had never dreamed that motherhood would be so taxing and she had nobody with whom to share her frustrations. Her own mother had died when she was but a girl and she rarely saw the sisters who had been so anxious to marry her off. Sowae, Sa Mi's sister-in-law, gushed about motherhood as if it was the best thing that could have ever happened. Sa Mi did not dare to mention the extent of her loneliness for fear of appearing ungrateful and inferior in her mothering.

Perhaps she was. She couldn't help feeling that she had been born without the mother gene. She presumed that she loved her children, every last one of them, but they also seemed so distant from her, as if they were not her own children at all, but that she had simply been the vessel through which God had decided to propagate the earth. All the children had their own distinct personalities, and each of them came into the world with the insecurities that she was a stranger to them too. The baby with whom she was struggling at the moment was prone to colicky outbursts and fussiness. He seemed to have come out of her womb with a general irritation and annoyance towards her. It was almost as if he could sense her doubts about motherhood and resented her from the day he was born. The sesame seed oil peddler's warning years ago about the complexity of loving one's own child had not been lost on Sa Mi. With all the strains and uncertainties of the times, Sa Mi felt she had nothing left to give to her children.

Soon, the oldest, was now fifteen, the same age that Sa Mi was when she had been promised to wed the second son of Yi *saboneem*. But unlike Sa Mi who was so childlike at that age, Soon had the cool detachment of a grown woman. Her suffering had etched a maturity to her disposition and a depth to her gaze. Now that she was a young woman, she took it upon herself to observe a cool distance from her father and stepmother.

Sa Mi neither noticed nor objected to her stepdaughter's detached manner. Instead, she sought to combat her own disappointments by leaving the house every chance she could get. Sa Mi made any excuse to go to the market where she would make her rounds throughout the neighborhood, stopping and saying "hello" to the other women and feeling somewhat satiated by the contact with other adults. There were no other alternatives for women like Sa Mi in those days and she took it upon herself to find small freedoms in her tiny existence.

Aside from excursions from the house, she still occasionally closed the rice paper screen of her bedroom and belted out the music of her soul. Her daughter Mijin, would listen on the other side and join in in perfect harmony.

Sa Mi had long abandoned her love of letters, though she did teach herself to speak Japanese perfectly and without an accent. She passed on this talent to Mijin much to her husband's dismay, "I don't know why you are wasting time with the oppressor's tongue, their days here are numbered." Sometimes Sa Mi would reply to her husband's remarks, miscalculating his short and acerbic temper, "But that is the language that our children will need to succeed, and besides, oppressors or not they are encroaching on all of Asia." Her husband, who lacked the virtue of patience, would lash out in anger, "Don't you see that they are all lies?! It is only a matter of time before Japan is toppled! Haven't you any convictions for your own country?!"

Sa Mi thought her husband's outbursts excessive, and throughout the years they had wounded her though she learned to live with them just as she learned to live with the trials of motherhood. Unlike her husband she was an unrelenting realist with her feet planted firmly on the ground. She had never known anything other than the Japanese occupation and she accepted that if Japan's rule was going to make up the background of her life, so be it. She would continue going to the market, staying out of the way of the military police, and obeying the laws of the land. As far as she was concerned, they would just have to make the best out of the situation. Isn't that what she had done with her husband's bad temper and his penchant for gambling? Isn't that what she had done with the children who scrambled around her house like strangers? The willfulness of her youth seemed like such a distant memory, and a futile one at that. Her fate in life was for her to be married, and that was exactly what happened to her, no matter her pain or her loss. Where she was once a jagged stone, her surface was now rounded out and smooth. This was the way of the world, and she could not understand her husband's passions when it came to issues as remote to them as politics. She assumed that the gulf between her and her husband was symbolic of their profoundly different positions. Sun was a man. He had the luxury of privilege to cushion his ideals. He had time to form his convictions, to cultivate and nurture them. These days, among the chaos of children, Sa Mi knew not even what she felt on most days.

When Sa Mi could no longer take the baby's screams she handed the child to a servant who often had better luck feeding him. She then continued to sit back and reflect.

It had been a turbulent year for her.

For one, it was the third year in a row that she had been wrong about the fall harvest. She had not only been wrong, she had been terribly mistaken. Earlier that year she kept delaying the farmers' eagerness to gather the melons and pumpkins saying that if they would wait just a few more weeks, they could double their yield. The tenant farmers whose lives lay so close to the earth, obeyed against their better instincts before an early frost came and ruined most of the crop. Sa Mi knew even before she had made the assertion that she had lost her talent for predicting the atmosphere's fickle rhythms. Unlike before, her senses now often felt numb and the weight of her indecision frightened her. She truly did not know, nor had any sense of what was going to happen next, with the atmosphere, with the crop, with anything. Perhaps her husband was right, perhaps she *had* lost her convictions, she had only wanted peace when there really was none to be had. So instead she allowed her mind to settle for the

112

illusions she had created about bending this way and that way in reaction to life's disappointments. Perhaps deep down she knew that if human beings twisted and turned too much to dodge what life had flung their way, their spines would become worn out altogether, until there was nothing left and nowhere to turn.

Her husband didn't even mention the ruined crop to her. She knew from her husband's increasingly intolerant temper that they had far more pressing financial issues to deal with. With the war stretching to the Pacific, they would be on an even tighter budget and expected to donate any surpluses of grain to the military. The fate of their country and the capriciousness of the climate were enough to put Sa Mi and her husband on alert. But their habits had become nestled too deep within them and they lacked the courage to confront the nuisance of truth.

For Sa Mi, material objects offered her solace and she often surrounded herself with finery as a kind of shelter from the uncertainties of her daily existence. She clothed her children in luxurious silks and strung gold around her own neck and wrists. They ate off treasured *celadon* porcelain from local artists of their region where the art form had flourished for centuries. Only the remnants of history survived for Sa Mi to admire. The collection of these items indulged Sa Mi's impeccable tastes and her appreciation for the humble curve of a one-of-a-kind vase or the sound of silver chopsticks clicking together or the delicate stitches of a silk tapestry gave her momentary reprieve from her anguish. Though she knew her tastes were far too extravagant given the reality of their financial situation and of the times, she found she simply could not part with her beloved trinkets. While she was well aware of the Buddhist concept of detachment, those objects struck such a chord with her she could not find herself able to separate her small life joys with those items of beauty. They offered her something motherhood could not.

For her husband, those coveted little collectibles made great gambling chips, and when he had to forfeit them, as he often did; Sun's guilt compelled him to replace the items two-fold to appease his wife and his own conscience. Together they collaborated in creating an even more uncertain future for their family, justifying to themselves that the uncertainty was imposed upon them, and not within their control. What were a few objects and some gambling losses here and there when Japan was ready to take over the world?

Sa Mi chuckled at how foolish she was as a young girl to think she could escape from Fate's omnipotent grasp. She had learned her lesson back then, running herself into a frenzy. And unlike her distraught husband who looked perpetually in pain as of late, Sa Mi took one breath at a time, believing that this was the way of life, to be subject to Fate's whim. There Sa Mi sat in contemplation among the growing number of strangers in her home, all of whom were born of their own hunger and desires.

The Expansion of Time

Even poetry did not offer Sun the solace he sought. To see his loneliness expressed in words, emptied onto a blank page gave him little comfort. The words felt empty, inadequate, and even though Sun hated to admit it, decadent. He had not picked up a pen since that day he saw his childhood friend carted off by the military police.

Sun fought to keep his mind from wandering to thoughts about the brutalities Childong may have been suffering; whether he was dead or holding fast to his remaining faculties somewhere in a dark cell. Sun had talked to Childong's sister several times who pleaded with him to find some way to seek information about her younger brother. But Sun had exhausted all of his possibilities. His friend, like many others, had simply vanished.

For Sun, the thrill of gambling filled the dull void in his heart and comforted him during uncertain times. Time moved quickly when he was throwing cards down on the table or clicking the *mahjong* tablets together. It was enough just to pass the time without letting his anxieties get the best of him. Gambling allowed Sun to let Time advance in its own determined and voracious manner, in the same way his wife took her long walks to the market. Outside these coveted routines, they allowed time to bottle up, to extend and to collapse again which served to magnify their loneliness.

Sun planned to use what was left of their money to placate the Japanese and find ways to steer their children away from trouble. Unlike his wife, he was wary of Japan's hold on power and even more jaded by their ways of attaining it. He knew only too well that the calls for young volunteers to support the war effort were all just a sham. Now that the war had reached the scale that it had, he knew that conscription was certain to follow, though the Japanese had already been shipping Koreans off to work in labor camps to remote areas in China.

His real concern in all this was for his oldest daughter who had reached that haunting age of seventeen. Words that had passed through many mouths and ears had reached him from Gyeungsong that his first and former lover – the child's mother – had continued to develop her taste for the mind-numbing narcotics that softened life's blows and that which claimed the life of her own mother. According to the rumors, it was in this sad and disillusioned state, alone and strung out, that Meeyoung was picked up by the Japanese police to support the war effort elsewhere. One could only imagine how a woman in such a state could work for the war other than to sexually service the lines of military men in some foreign and frightening environment. Sun shuddered at the thought of such cruelty and the foolhardiness of his once naïve and innocent heart. Did he have a hand in her tragic fate?

He crushed the stub of his cigarette and let out a guttural sigh. All he could think of dealing with now was the fate of the daughter whose future he *could* influence, and he made his charitable rounds to the Japanese offices to be sure that she was not being considered for any kind of labor. The only exemptions that were permitted was if she was already working for the war effort, which was a slap in the face for Koreans like Sun who believed that no proper young woman should be allowed to leave the house until she was married. Marriage was the other exemption, and though he had been talking to others about such a possibility, he knew it would be a few years before such an agreement would be fulfilled. In the meantime, he had to be sure that he was not met with any unwelcome surprises, so he satiated the greedy hands of the local military officers to ensure the safety of his daughter Soon.

Meanwhile, Soon resented her father and the home where she had been abandoned too vehemently to notice what Sun was up to. Had she known, it would not have made any difference, for she would have preferred to be shipped away to save her from her solitude. Soon felt alienated from her own siblings all her life and even more so from her stepmother who barely had enough maternal instincts to mother her own children, much less her. But it was her father whom she loathed the most. Soon didn't bother to explore what was at the root of her resentment, she only knew that she blamed him for all the miseries she had suffered thus far in life.

The girls at school who envied her flawless skin and haughty air, ridiculed her behind her back as everyone knew from the gossip of the adults that she was a product of her parents' youthful carelessness, and not a legitimate Yi like her brothers and sister. This day, like most, she took her lunch alone at school. Like for most girls of privilege at her school, a servant brought her food piping hot from home, filled with the tastiest delicacies.

"At least she can cook," Soon thought to herself as she picked at the fragrant marinated beef and the perfectly fermented *kimchi* with her chopsticks. She was never very impressed by her stepmother whose talent for pulling together a mouth-watering meal was something Soon's pride never allowed her to fully appreciate. Instead she idly picked at her food with her chopsticks until she lost her appetite completely. Soon was easily annoyed by her stepmother who she thought was a model pushover for her husband and kids. She couldn't feel hurt from any attention she was denied from her, for Sa Mi was not much different with the mothering of her own children who she hastily handed to the servants when they began to get too fussy and whose whims she easily gave into as to not have to deal with the bother of disciplining or challenging them. Soon took it as her own personal rebellion to not finish all of the food her stepmother had packed for her. She felt a certain self-satisfaction when she went home and her stepmother would ask her, "You barely touched your food. Was everything okay with it?" Frustrated, she would then turn away clicking her tongue. Soon reveled in those rare moments when her stepmother would express her care and passions, though it was usually only through her cooking.

This was the same woman who would not know to pick up and soothe a child when he came to her crying with a scraped knee, but if you rejected her cooking, she took immediate offense. Soon picked at her food just to get a rise out of her stepmother, it reminded her that this one mother figure in her life was still alive. Most of the time she observed her stepmother as impassive and undemonstrative to the children that wreaked havoc around her. Sa Mi sat around during those days in a blank stupefaction as if she was miscast in her role as mother and wife, though her eyes lit up every now and then when she was furiously assembling meals in the kitchen or admiring some gem or porcelain piece that Soon's father had brought home for her, or when she bolted out of the house in desperation to escape the routines of the home.

Soon's criticisms of her stepmother allowed her to keep her thoughts of her real mother at bay. As much as people would have liked to believe, she was not immune to their harsh words and gossip. She knew from all the whispers around her that her mother was not an "honorable" woman, and for whatever reason, was "unfit" to marry her father. And Soon's pride was too great to ask her father about her. Instead, she kept everything bottled up behind an impertinent demeanor that intimidated all her classmates and prevented her from making any friends. She preferred it that way. The less people meddled in her personal affairs the better. It seemed that the only thing adults were capable of were pity or contempt, which were really the same thing in her eyes.

There was however, one adult who treated her with neither pity nor contempt, but rather with a simple raw instinct that was honest and forthright. He was the high school music teacher who was fresh out of college; lanky, with a long face and demeanor, and worst of all, Japanese. Unlike the young Korean English teacher who made all the girls swoon with his rolling pronunciations of English phrases that the girls didn't bother to understand, Mr. Takayama was not someone with whom anybody wasted their time. It was not that he was particularly bad looking, but rather that he had a tendency to slip past you unnoticed. He was that negligible in appearance. This was a challenging position to be in as a teacher where success relies on your ability to command an audience, but Mr. Takayama simply stepped aside to the music he played on the gramophone. His tastes betrayed his inconsequential appearance.

Throughout the whole class period, from beginning to end with few words in between, Mr. Takayama would turn on the gramophone to the haunting harmonic ruptures of Wagner, the rhythmic clashes of Vivaldi, and he would end always with the bloodshed of Beethoven's Symphony no. 9. His head would nod violently to the stark contrasts of the music as if his neck was made of springs that could anticipate each movement of the composition. His hair, which lacked any personality when the music was off, would dance desperately on top of his head, and his whole façade took on a disheveled, unkempt, and peculiar appearance. If it had been anyone else standing before the class jerking and convulsing to Vivaldi's *The Four Seasons*, the spectacle might have possessed the quality of intrigue, but with Mr. Takayama the experience was wholly strange and bizarre. A palpable silence fell over the room when the music erupted and the teenage girls would shrink into their seats as their teacher trembled as if possessed by the violins, before he pushed his satiated hair back into place. Not only did it feel inappropriate given the times – with a bloody war and a dire political situation – but the music itself felt like an assault, as if this Japanese teacher was using it to arouse the passions in the young girls' hearts.

Soon was neither titillated nor offended by Takayama's display. She was rather more amused and curious of his oddities. Not even the powerful movements of Wagner could penetrate the haughtiness of her demeanor, though even she would admit that the music struck a chord with her. Its affect was jarring compared to the familiar gut-wrenching *arias* of the *pansori* whose singers were trained to tear their vocal chords to approximate the depths of suffering in their tortured voices. Even the ancient court music with the resonant gongs of the *pyon-gyong* echoed the hollow sounds of tragedy. These new sounds however, were an assault against suffering itself.

Whenever her stepmother closed the door to her bedroom to unleash the anguish in her heart through song, or when her younger sister who inherited her mother's lovely voice would harmonize along with her, Soon would reach for the nearest pillow to cover her ears in disgust. It was always the same song, the same story, the same lonely melody of suffering and she hated it as much as she hated the looks of pity that were cast upon her. The sounds that burst out of the gramophone were entirely different. They lifted their way up as if of their own accord, exploding and colliding without any care or acknowledgement to pain or pity. Soon was enraptured by it, that is, as much as her stony disposition would allow.

So it was in this manner that Soon took the opportunity to stir up the boredom in her life and in her own way, fire back at her father who returned her cries as a child with looks of pity and despair. To make matters more interesting, she decided to keep her secret to herself. It had more power that way and she craved that authority when it came to matters of the heart. She promised herself that she would never let her father's past mistakes (least of all his role in conceiving her) cause her any more pain as an adult. She would be sure of that. If she initiated the first attack, neither he nor anyone else could stake claim of pitying or shaming her. Every time her father would look at her with that guilt-ridden face, she would laugh to herself and call him a fool, for he had no reason to pity her at all. Soon had too much confidence in her own beauty to think that getting to Mr. Takayama would pose any kind of challenge, she could tell from the spring in his neck that he was waiting for someone like her to pounce on him. The conquest would be all hers. Satisfied with herself, Soon clicked her chopsticks together and took one luscious piece of meat to her mouth before she closed her lunchbox for her stepmother to open later in disappointment. Before she and this Japanese teacher had exchanged even one word, she had the course of the relationship all mapped out.

While Soon was planning her affair with the eccentric Japanese music teacher, her father was lighting a fresh cigarette, plotting out ways to protect this very daughter and to keep her away from the wrath of the Japanese.

There Sun sat at the table with a possessed look of desperation. One lucky day a few months ago had inspired a streak in him at the *mah-jong* table. The luck hadn't lasted however, and before he knew it he had started putting plots of his land on the table, thinking that the spirits of his deceased parents would protect him. They did not. And before he knew it an acre here and an acre there had vanished into thin air. As panic set in, he then started borrowing chips from the loan sharks who were affiliated with the gambling hall. His years of drowning his sorrows away with the thrill of chance had finally compelled him to do the inconceivable. If he thought about it too much he could not live with the disappointment that he had dug a grave hole for his family, so instead of thinking he fought desperately to dig himself out, but the more he dug the deeper he drowned.

He felt like a slave. A slave to the Japanese and their gross humiliations; a slave to a world that allowed such injustice, whose palpable uncertainty hung to his shoulders like vultures gnawing on his back; and a slave to his miserable habit that embodied everything about the emerging world order that he abhorred. It was a world that privileged providence over tradition, and caprice over substance. Who was he to think that he could play at this new table? Gambling had always been a past time for him, a leisurely hobby that brought people together to share laughs and stories. Nobody really lost anything significant. They always had their pride to fall back on and another day to look forward to. But these days he could not help but notice the grittiness of his plight, or the diseased look of desperation that plagued him wherever he turned. He saw it when he looked in the mirror and he was ashamed. He was ashamed of what he had become.

In that moment, Sun tried to come to terms with what everyone else in town was beginning to whisper about: the Yi family – whose gilded history was one of local lore, and whose ancestry hovered over their ten thousand acres and their grand estate – had gone broke.

Soonjin and Takayama

He turned out to be surprisingly tender in bed. A generous lover. She was but a child when she reached out for his hand and peered into his eyes one day after all the other girls had bolted out of his classroom. Her teacher justified his actions by asserting her command of the situation. Clearly, she was anything but inexperienced. *She* had seduced *him* after all. He had simply acquiesced. Japanese girls would never be so bold. Perhaps it was true what they said about these Koreans. At first, Takayama did not know how to take the yearning gaze from his student Soon, but instinct soon set in and the two found themselves entangled in each other's arms every moment they could find.

"*Like that*," whispered Soon into his ear, barely words, but more like a needful breath of encouragement, as if her very existence depended on the stroke of his skin against hers. Takayama said nothing. Never one for many words, he was ever more taciturn with his young lover, but no less expressive.

Aside from the faint whispers and moans that he elicited from her, in short declarative sentences Soon confided in

Takayama. And though Soon spoke perfect Japanese, she spoke to him only Korean:

"My father, he has lost everything."

Takayama responded by gently stroking the side of her cheek, running the tip of his finger over her neck and shoulder, down toward the peeks of her nipples.

"They are so foolish, both of them," inhaled Soon as Takayama's hand reached down toward her naval. "They haven't a clue of how to live."

The normally stony disposition hid nothing in front of her lover, "what will you do?" she asked in stilted whispers as his lips brushed every square inch of her neck, "when Japan surrenders?"

Takayama paused to look into Soon's eyes. For someone who passed not even one Korean word from his lips, he seemed to understand better than any native speaker. Instead of responding with words, after staring searchingly into his lover's eyes, Takayama proceeded to caress her supple skin with his lips, moving ever downward on her body.

Soon groaned with pleasure before reaching for Takayama's face, the sharp angles of his jawline nestled within her delicate fingers. She brought his face to hers and with a tenderness she did not know she was capable of she said, "They will kill you. If Japan surrenders, they will kill you. You know this, right?" she asked, her words, slow and measured.

Takayama let his face rest in her hands, then dropped his forehead between her breasts and explored her nipples with the tip of his tongue. His fingers plunged into her as he felt her tremble beneath him.

Clutching onto Takayama, Soon reverted back to her choked whispers, her fingernails digging into his back, unable to contain herself.

"You won't make it out alive," she breathed into his ear, one hand gripping his thick hair, the other hand squeezing his back.

As Takayama penetrated her, Soon bit into his shoulder, her bodily pleasure and the depths of her loneliness colliding.

Afterward, they lied in silence until Takayama, still not having said one word, reached over for a cigarette, without managing to disentangle himself from Soon.

Rolling over onto her side to face him Soon asked, "Why are you still here? It's not safe."

Takayama took slow, deep drags from his cigarette as Soon lied on her side watching him. Then putting it out, he took her into his arms once again.

They spent the better part of the winter and spring of 1942 in this manner. Soon and Takayama made love as the world around them went up in smoke. It was unclear what motivated Soon to insist on the possibility of Japan's defeat and Takayama's vulnerability should the war end. The only news she ever heard was controlled by the colonial government which praised the empire's victories. One could only assume that it was her nationalist impulse that compelled her to toy with Takayama in such a manner. It was perhaps the same satisfaction she derived from whispering sexual commands in his ear in Korean. Whatever the reason, the prescience of Soon's warnings appeared to be almost orchestrated.

Other than proceeding to make love to her with tenderness and zeal, Takayama never responded verbally to Soon's warnings. And like the empire herself, Takayama did not budge. It was just their way of communicating, something that Sa Mi discovered one day while removing Soon's lunch pack from her bag and finding slips of paper that said things like:

"You must return. This will not go on much longer." [In Korean.]

"My place. 7:30p study group." [In Japanese, different handwriting.]

"You are foolish to stay here." [Korean]

"Come to me. Now." [Japanese]

"Go back to Japan." [Korean]

"I need you." [Japanese]

Sa Mi tore up the messages into tiny pieces and threw them into the fire without confronting her stepdaughter, though the shock of those notes diminished any shred of sympathy for the child she raised from the day she was left on Sa Mi's doorstep. In Sa Mi's eyes, the slips of paper proved that the impudent girl would only sully her husband's good name. Sa Mi had to be sure that Sun married her off and soon, lest the whole family be buried in further scandal.

And just as Soon had warned, one hot, barren day, three years later, Japan surrendered.

Takayama never left the peninsula. But when he walked out the door of his home one day in mid-August 1945, he didn't quite get as far as the school before he was attacked and brutally killed by a group of nationalists formed from the ensuing chaos and violence.

The news eventually reached Soon. And if anyone paid attention to her, which no one did, they might have detected an iridescent sphere forming in the far reaches of Soon's eyelid. Was it a tear? We will never know, for she blinked and it disappeared, only to be replaced with her signature stony disposition.

Bong-jin

Sun sat at the table, a possessed look of desperation piercing from his eyes.

Everything appeared to him as an omen, and his current state propelled an even quicker temper in the already hot-blooded Sun. When his daughter was born with locks of curls, he blamed her cursed curly head of hair for boding his losing streak. And when they heard the sound of their father at the gate, all his children scurried away like mice, knowing Sun's meticulous nature and fearing his wrath, which lately had become magnified.

It was of little use however, lately there was nothing that Sun detested more than disobedient children. He loathed those that had no control of their vices, who allowed their passions to rule their minds. Sun hated it as much as he hated his own present situation. But even in his most desperate moments he never allowed his pride to escape him. He never lost control of his drinking and he was known for his punctuality and timeliness. When Yi Sun Soo said he was going to be somewhere at a certain time, he never backed out on his word. And regardless of his business outside of the house, he always came back to his family. He expected nothing less from his children and wondered how some of them turned out to be so different from him, he wondered how their genetic make-up could be so foreign. He felt this most palpably with his first-born son, the *changnam* of the family, and the one out of the children who felt his father's wrath the most frequently of all.

Bong-jin was a child who was loved by everyone except his father. He was affectionate and warm-hearted with his younger siblings, popular and well-liked among his peers, and adored by his mother. At sixteen, his height and strapping good looks won him the favor of anybody that came his way, and for those who needed a little more prodding, his charm could melt the coldest of hearts. What irritated his father to no end however was the fact that Sun knew that no amount of charm could substitute for a sense of responsibility. Responsibility was what made one a man, charm simply made one a ladies' man. Sun could see that his son still had a lot of growing up to do and he blamed his wife for spoiling their first-born.

"How is he going to make a life for himself like *that*?" he asked his wife pointedly as they observed their son near the house, socializing with friends.

"*Bong-jin-ya*!!" he called out to him sternly.

"Leave him alone!" Sa Mi responded, frustrated with her husband's cruelty as of late. "Let him be so he can talk to his friends," she pleaded. But Sun had one hand on his hip and fury in his eyes as the defeated son started walking his way.

"Do you know what time it is right now?" Sun asked the child with irritation.

"No, I'm not sure father," the boy responded with his head down.

"It's after seven right now," Sun replied accusingly.

"Yes father."

"What time did I ask you to be home?"

"Sorry father, I lost track of time."

"Sorry, huh?"

These were the last civil words that were spoken before Sun erupted into his fiery temper which made the children in the house run for cover and even caused his wife to cower. Screaming every insult he could hurl at this useless son of his, he finally ended with his classic phrase, "When are you going to grow up anyway? Wake up and be an adult!" he shouted, flinging a cold slap across his son's face before walking away. The children were too young to understand that Sun was really screaming at himself.

But no matter how many episodes like this passed and no matter how many times Sun shouted at his son to "wake up and be an adult," Bong-jin always remained the same, easy-going to the point of exhaustion. The truth was, Sun really needed his oldest to step up to fulfill his role as *changnam*. To act as the pillar of the family, to assume responsibility for the family's legacy, to know to take care of his parents. But one could not beat filial piety into a child. After all, it was the *changnam* who was to perform the ancestral rites for the family, and the *changnam* who would take care of the parents and younger siblings in the future when times became rough.

Sun knew that the times were changing and that he had nothing to give to his first-born, unlike the land he had inherited from his own parents. The world they were coming upon was a new one, family names were becoming less important than knowing how to survive, having the skills to survive, and possessing the courage to face up to the coarse and unforgiving caprices of the world. Sun knew that the only skills he could offer his children during changing times were a sense of responsibility and a drive toward ambition. Though he could only direct his own ambitions toward the gambling table, he hoped that his children could discover more in this new world of theirs, a world he felt too old, too far beyond the times to understand. What good was a poet during uncertain times? No better than his wife perhaps, who had the voice of an angel. They came from the class whose talents needed no monetary compensation, not the class of artists who entertained for a *won* note. Sun had many pressing things on his mind and he needed the reassurance, the security of his eldest son to help lead the family. It was a reassurance he would not get. A kind and generous heart with nothing else to stand on was a liability in this new world. Sun surmised that his son would never survive on his own, much less, help the rest of his family.

Instead, Sun worked without delay to marry off his oldest daughter so he could then marry his son off to a girl from a well-to-do family (it was considered bad luck to make wedding arrangements for a younger sibling before an older one). Soon, who was by then bored with the Japanese music teacher, broke off their affair. She would find out later that he had been brutally killed shortly after the liberation of the peninsula, when he got caught in a crowd celebrating Japan's defeat. When she walked down the aisle with her father by her side and he still wore that look of pity he saved only for her, she gloated in self-satisfaction. "He thinks he is so smart," she thought to herself, glancing at her father in disgust. "Really, he knows nothing of me." Her stepmother, who had been apprised of Soon's antics, did not dare to mention any of it to her husband who would not tolerate any negative talk about Soon, "It is not her fault," he would say to whatever offense reached his ears, letting out a regretful sigh.

He felt good, at least, that he had been able to marry her to a decent family. Sun had actually done quite well with seeking a mate for this daughter who was cursed by the brand of illegitimacy. Soon's new husband was quickly ascending the ranks in the military and was following his father's footsteps as a sharp and well-respected officer.

For his useless son, Sun sought a daughter-in-law who was older and who could compensate for all of his son's liabilities. He found her in an upstanding family, who had the means to educate their daughter (they had no sons for whom an education would be of better use), to be a medical doctor. She was as homely as a duck and possessed a disposition that was as equally unattractive. If she knew how to smile she did not show it, nor did she seem very impressed by her new husband's charms. Sun thought she would be the perfect choice for his son Bong-jin. She likely would not tolerate his charming ways, and if he could not follow through with his financial responsibility, at least she possessed the skills of a medical doctor.

His wife had fought him all the way, "how could you marry our fine son to *that*?!" she had asked, weeping into her handkerchief. But Sun did not budge once he made a decision and he had already made up his mind. Sa Mi wept through the entire ceremony and everyone knew they were not tears of joy. There had been many other candidates who had been vying for his son's attention, all of whom were young, beautiful, and graceful, but Sun rejected all of them. And when their families attended the wedding, it took everything for them not to weep into their handkerchiefs as well.

If the sentiment of the wedding was any indication of how the young couple would embark on their new lives together, it did not bode well for them. The good-natured Bong-jin did as he always did, he entrusted himself to the whims of his father and hoped for the success that would inspire the love he so desperately craved from Sun.

Mijin

B y 1944, Mijin sensed the tensions in her family. As the oldest (legitimate) daughter she was the object of her parents' spoils and affections. She received no looks of pity from anyone for she was born with a stamp of entitlement that her older sister had been denied. She was rather more like her mother's companion than she was her daughter, and the two women discussed their feelings and thoughts openly and laughed together like sisters. The traits and dispositions that she had inherited from her mother had been nurtured by benefit of her privileged position. Like her mother, Mijin possessed a love of music and was gifted with an angelic voice which she cultivated through private music lessons. Her fingers danced along the piano keys and the bowed lute creating soulful melodies.

Mijin's cultivated eye for the finer things in life was also a trait she had adopted from her mother, and together they passed many hours at artisan shops and stores indulging their shared love of the pieces of art and objects that made their souls stir.

For Mijin, these privileges were not viewed as mere fancies so much as they were steadfast pillars of her existence, which was, for the most part, carefree, indulgent, and by all means happy. The girls she went to school with shared the joys of their status, and, as is often the case of those for whom material comfort is a way of life, they took much of their entitlements for granted.

Mijin, who was soon to reach her eighteenth birthday, had spent so much of her life immersed in material comforts that they became of such monumental importance she couldn't find herself able to give them up when she saw her family falling onto hard times. Those creature comforts had become larger than life itself. She thought not about the fate of her younger siblings when her father's estate started to crumble but was desperate to figure out how she could save those objects that had brought her so much joy.

This was all that occupied her mind one day as she hurried home from the artisan store where she had her eye on a glimmering jewelry box made of smooth black lacquer and intricate designs inlaid with mother of pearl. Just seeing it there had brought her so much solace!

Though the seduction of music was always on her mind, when Mijin walked swiftly home that day from the store, her thoughts were centered around the exquisite jewelry box she had just seen and for once in her life, didn't have the money to purchase. She hadn't liked that feeling of unfulfilled desire gnawing at the pit of her stomach. She hadn't liked it at all and she could only hope that the rough times that had seized her parents were soon to pass. They had appeared particularly anxious and withdrawn as of late, especially her father who she would catch a glimpse of in the middle of the night, still awake, smoking Japanese cigarettes alone underneath the stars. Everything pointed to the fact that things were quite grim. Her mother had already given up her most valuable pieces of jewelry and all other precious items in the house. Though her father was quick to replace such valuables with something else pleasing to the eye, nothing new had been brought into the home for quite some time.

One day, the stark reality seized Mijin: right there before her very eyes, their house appeared to be stripped bare. Nobody said anything about the disappearing remnants of their lives, and the silence that surrounded the growing void was palpable. The boundaries of their estate quickly began to shrink as loan sharks collected on their debt. Still, like everyone else in her family whose denial was just as tragic as their plight, Mijin leaned on the possibility that this was all just a passing era and that things would get back to normal soon enough. Her parents had not asked her to give up her precious items and her jewelry, not because they couldn't use them, but their pride would not allow them. Nonetheless, Mijin hoarded those items and guarded them with her life in the event that her parents might grow desperate enough to ask her for them.

The reality was, neither parent could deny their daughter anything and if this meant making the foolish decision to get her the jewelry box that had moved her heart so much – even though the foundation on which they dwelled was crumbling – they would find a way to make their daughter happy. Mijin only knew too well the weakness her parents shared towards her and it was with this knowledge that she quickly walked home to relay her desperation for the beloved jewelry box to her parents.

She was just a few blocks short of the estate when she was assaulted in her tracks.

"Excuse me miss," someone called from behind her, "excuse me!"

Startled, Mijin kept walking at her pace, embarrassed that she had made the decision to walk to town by herself. Her parents had told her several times that only certain "types" of unmarried, single young women walked around unescorted. She thought they were so old-fashioned.

When she heard a male voice say "excuse me" one more time she abruptly turned around to face her perpetrator.

The sounds of the gramophone with the sultry voice of a jazz singer quickly flooded her ears when her eyes met and locked with the tall, fine-looking young man that stood in front of her. Mijin quickly cast her eyes down to observe the modesty of the times. She wondered if he could see her heart racing out of her chest, for she could feel his own breathlessness and the heat emanating from his body. She had never been this close to any man before, with the exception of her father and brothers. It was thrilling and nerve-wracking all at the same time.

As Mijin continued to stare at the ground, the young man started in his soothing voice, "I'm so sorry to have startled you. You see I've been chasing after you for quite some time, I noticed that you must be in a hurry. I also noticed that you dropped this," and with both of his hands he respectfully presented Mijin's scarf to her.

Still looking down, Mijin bowed and received the scarf with both hands, "Yes, it is mine, thank you," she replied.

The young woman's beauty had not escaped him and he stood awkwardly searching for something to say before he blurted out his name and bowed, "Kim Ju Won," he declared, "I live just a few miles in the other direction," he indicated with a show of his hands.

"Yi Mijin," the young woman replied with a bow. The town was small and her father was an important figure, she knew he would figure out who she was just by her last name. She knew immediately who his father was when he said his.

As they both stood awkwardly at the side of the road, she staring at the dirt, he trying to steal glances of her beautiful face, he followed up his introduction with, "It is such a lovely scarf, but it hardly competes with the beauty of its owner."

This was almost too much for Mijin as she felt not only like she could belt out the lyrics of the love songs she played over and over again on her gramophone, but that she embodied the music itself, as if her entire being was immersed in its rhythms and melodies.

Not knowing how to react, Mijin quickly bowed one last time and then turned around toward the direction of her estate. The charming English teacher stared after her, wondering when their paths would meet again.

When Mijin made it home she was bubbling over with excitement, the precious jewelry box that had been her sole focus of the day was now but a distant memory. Instead, she called out to her mother in desperation to share with her the news of her blissful encounter.

Time Collapses

Sun was at his lowest. Unable to accept that his life, indeed that his whole world was crumbling away right from under him, he desperately found himself at the gambling houses at all hours of the night trying to win back his livelihood. Local Japanese officials who had also received wind of the yangban's vulnerabilities, seized the opportunity to strip him of the greater share of his property. Knowing that Sun had run dry of bribes, corrupt government officials conspired with the owners of the gambling houses to manufacture false papers showing that Sun had reneged on his loans and was therefore required to give up his land holdings. The government awarded the owners of the gambling houses with a hefty payoff and a promise to stay away from their business operations while the government inherited a prosperous, expansive plot of land. They rejoiced in the success of their operation as well as their victim's suffering, for whom they had to go to great lengths and measures to harm given his position of power and wealth.

Sun argued his case, refuting the veracity of the documents and demanding that his property be rightfully returned. One high official who had lived for this very day took arrogant bull-legged strides toward Sun with his oversized military boots, inhaled one last drag from his cigarette, and crushed the stub with his boot.

"Do I hear you have a complaint in this matter *josaengjin*?" he declared, staring at the dignified man like a squashed bug.

"What has happened to me is not right. Please, these charges against me are completely false," knowing by then that he was helpless in the matter.

"Are you calling me a liar? Are you charging that this great government who has taken care of you and sought to civilize your despicable race, lied? That smacks of slander to me, doesn't it gentlemen?" he inquired to the group of his men who affirmed him in unison like well-programmed robots. "As a matter of fact, that sounds a lot like treason to me, doesn't it to you *saboneem*? Tell me, do you happen to know what the punishment is for treason? It seems to have escaped me," then a horrible roar came out of his belly which erupted into a laugh supported by the chuckles of his robotic background. Sun's anger which pulsated into every vein and every artery in his body was exploding inside of him, but against his raging instincts, Sun remained silent.

As abruptly as it had begun, the round-bellied official stopped laughing and narrowed his eyes at Sun, "Stay away from here," he seethed, "and if I hear from anyone that you spoke of this matter again I will have you charged with treason so fast you will not even be able to say goodbye to your family."

Sun only knew too well that the abundant flesh that stood before him was quite capable of following through with such a charge and seeing that he had no other choice, he looked into each of the faces who sought to humiliate him (most of whom who would not look at him, but stared straight ahead into nothing), and he walked away.

When he walked into his house, his wife set aside her crochet needles to greet him. A simple wave of his hand as he proceeded to the courtyard indicated that he was not interested in conversation, or much else for that matter, as he hurried passed Sa Mi.

Sa Mi knew about the charges against her husband and she also knew that while they may have been fabricated, her husband proved to be an easy target with his reckless ways. She could never understand this weakness in him for it contradicted his character in every way. Sun was meticulous in every other aspect of his life. He recorded every transaction he ever made and every loan he took out, recording the name of the lender, amount, interest rate, date, and due date. And though their rate of payment combined with astronomical interest rates held no hope of their ever paying off their debt in this lifetime, her husband was still able to manage the debt in the sense that he knew exactly where he stood with each loan collector. It was not that his meticulousness when it came to such matters made any difference when it came to their futures, but it did somewhat absolve him of culpability in Sa Mi's eyes, where she felt the Japanese government had taken advantage of her husband's weaknesses.

Still, it was her husband's behavior that gave rise to their current demise. The government had simply helped the process along. But they didn't talk about such matters, perhaps hoping that if they didn't mention it, it might simply go away. This was unfortunately not the case, and in their silence they fell deeper and deeper into duress.

Sa Mi distracted herself with Mijin's upcoming wedding. In light of their financial situation, Sa Mi swiftly made wedding arrangements for the end of the summer to wed their daughter to the nice-looking and well-mannered English teacher. He would make a fine son-in-law and Sa Mi had never seen her daughter so happy. Engulfed in the throes of young love, Mijin could talk, think, dream about nothing but her upcoming wedding. She had all but forgotten about her love affair with material objects and replaced her worship with the man who had interrupted her thoughts one lovely summer day. Not fully aware of the extent of the financial tragedy that was looming over the young girl's household, the parents of the English teacher also approved of the union. So as her husband wallowed in despair, Sa Mi busily made arrangements for her daughter, thinking more than once of her own experiences of being wed many years ago. Who could have predicted how her life would unfold?

Yeonjin: A Side Story of Love and Death

A result of the time the two families spent together was the formation of an indelible bond between Sa Mi's daughter Mijin, and her often ignored cousin, Yeonjin. Though Yeon was two years older than Mijin, they got along like best friends and were more like sisters than either one became with their own sisters. Mijin followed Yeon around affectionately calling her eonni, the term used by younger girls to address older girls and literally meaning "big sister."

It was a joyful haven of friendship for both girls. Sa Mi's daughter Mijin, idolized her cousin's legendary beauty, grace, and generosity, and her cousin valued Mijin's excellent taste, sharp wit, and attentive ear. An attentive ear was something that Yeon lacked in her life. Unlike the close relationship that Mijin shared with Sa Mi, who became more like friends than mother and daughter, Yeon was virtually ignored by her mother. Yeon's father, the rare moments when she got to see him, acknowledged her in his detached and aloof way which only fueled his wife's jealousy. Though it was customary in those days for mothers to favor their sons, the disparity between Sowae's total preoccupation for her son and her complete disregard of her daughter, was a sorrowful sight even to the most society-abiding citizens. Even in front of Sa Mi with whom she exaggerated at great lengths about her children's accomplishments, Sowae was always critical of her oldest daughter and admitted that Yeon's presence unsettled her.

"Even the way she looks at me sometimes, I feel she is trying to peer inside of me. She is too smart for her own good. It is unbecoming of young girls."

It was true that Yeon had a reticent, thoughtful disposition. After all, she was as her mother had correctly surmised, extremely intelligent. Like her chagun-oma[2] Sa Mi, Yeon had a hunger for knowledge and nourished herself with study, books, and school to compensate for the lack of attention she received at home. Sa Mi empathized with her niece and recalled her now distant memories of going to school and her own mother's sacrifices to allow her to continue her education. She thought back on those times with an empty longing, but with a grounded sense of reality that she was where she was at that moment as a matter of destiny. It was Sa Mi that convinced her sister-in-law to allow Yeon to continue her education.

"You may think it is unbecoming, but a woman should also have her own mind and thoughts to lean back on. You must encourage her every moment you have. Besides, it may enhance her father's position."

Her sister-in-law paid no heed to Sa Mi's expressions of concern for her daughter's well-being but deferred to the norm of her social status which was to decorate their children with education to further separate themselves from others who did not have the resources to do so. Sowae also didn't object because she reasoned that keeping the child in school and busy with activity, allowed for less awkward moments between them. Yeon sailed through her studies, always landing first in her class and winning popularity among her schoolmates. When it came time for college pursuits, her parents decided that pharmacy was an appropriate

---

[2] Father's younger brother's wife.

field of study for a young woman, (though actual professional practice would be unlikely because they would have found her a mate by the time she graduated, and she too, like Sa Mi, would have to abandon her scholarly pursuits for domesticity).

Yeon was well aware of this inescapable reality. She had witnessed it herself with all the women that came before her and learned early on that her existence and everything that surrounded it was devoted to maintaining appearances and ensuring the re-election of her father to his esteemed post. She fulfilled her role dutifully by doing what was expected of her. She was, by all means, an exemplary daughter: regal in stature, pious toward her parents, and as much envy as she evoked from her peers, even the most jealous of hearts were eventually won over by her generosity and charm. But no matter how much admiration and respect she commanded, she could not win the favor of her own mother. Her mother's feelings toward her were so indifferent that Sowae never wasted a breath to raise her voice at Yeon or to tell her anything at all for that matter. Not that anything Yeon did warranted a scolding, but in her mother's eyes, she was not even worthy of being a whipping post like some daughters were to their mothers in a strange, twisted show of affection. The resentful woman simply ignored Yeon and spoke to her only when it was absolutely necessary which she did tersely and devoid of emotion.

The time came when Yeon reached that age when everyone's energies are focused around one's marriage prospects. For Yeon these possibilities were endless due to the admirers who prostrated themselves before her father just to catch a glimpse of her graceful beauty. If the potential mates served no political end they were quickly and summarily dismissed.

By this time, Japan had suffered a devastation that would change the history of the world forever, as lives were incinerated into a mushroom cloud. The Japanese had fled that lonely peninsula jutting defiantly out into the sea, and the Americans quickly occupied the country for fear that the Russians would beat them to it. The reluctant allies then decided to sever the peninsula at the thirty-eighth parallel in order to preserve the capital Gyeungsong and renamed it Seoul under the purview of the United States.

With tragedy comes opportunity, and for one's political career it was a critical moment in history. Yeon's father and Sa Mi's brother-in-law, had by then elbowed his way among other political aspirants to the new South Korean regime and was advancing quickly in the established government. The paranoia of the times had called into question his so-called "centrist" views at a moment when one was forced to choose between one extreme or the other, and any claims toward moderation was held in suspicion by both sides; these indecisive, noncommittal traitors were quickly eliminated if not by the communists, certainly by the rightist regime that the United States was molding in South Korea. His daughter's marriage was too attractive of an opportunity for the struggling politician to appease his opponents and to seal his political future.

Yeon's father found the answer to his troubles in a certain Colonel Im In Won. Colonel Im was a young army officer who had catapulted through the military ranks by virtue of his impeccable fighting skills and his relentless driving will. The mystery surrounding the details of his past did nothing to hinder his status as a symbol for the budding anti-communist South Korean regime where he had become quite a celebrity. His widely-known tale of propaganda glory went something like this:

Grew up in poverty somewhere in the North where he was subjected to the cruel, violent insurrections of an inchoate Comintern-supported leftist movement. Two younger brothers swept into the movement out of threats on their lives. Parents slaughtered by the Japanese. The colonel, with a burning hunger for democracy and freedom from both tyrants, that is, the Communists and the Japanese, fled in search of freedom.

This was the story they used in the media, and the one that won him popularity among the people. But then of course, there was the other story, the one that the public did not know.

He grew up in the unforgiving climate of the North Korean town of Kanggye, near the China border, and his face reflected every last bitterness and harshness of his suffering. Colonel Im's family had been tenant farmers, working that stubborn, arid land that refused to sprout life even under the most benign environmental conditions. He had grown up in and experienced the misery of the feudal landowning system that relegated him and his family to virtual serfdom to the wealthy landowners. The only thing that barren land was fertile in producing was the seeds of leftist ideology that germinated and bloomed into the sweetest smelling buds of hope – elevating toward the heavens and opening its petals in liberation. The syrupy smell of communism permeated the air, but its intoxicating scent was a mismatch with the choppy sounds of emerging leaders whose desperate voices shouted into the megaphone, eliciting cries of joy from the audience.

To Im, the demagoguery of the performances was something different than the ideas, and a theater in and of itself. And unlike his family and virtually everyone in the town who had revolted against their oppressive landowners, he was unimpressed by shows of emotion and suspicious of those who provoked them. The government had its own suspicions and before anything could come of their emotional demonstrations the leftist agitators were quickly quelled by the colonial government.

The military was in the cards for the colonel early on with its reliance on order and structure and its detachment from the emotions that complicate the real goals and objectives of life. So, when he and his younger brothers began to attend the covert gatherings where they accepted grain stamped by the Comintern, he was never quite comfortable with the excessive shouting and exaggerated waving of hands expounded by some of its short-lived leaders who fervently declared that they must take up arms in the face of the enemy. Still, he wondered if this was the only way out of their plight and leaned toward it for it was the only option available.

Someone must have read his mind and saw that he was not entirely convinced. The colonel was never demonstrative. It was not in his character to be expressive. This stoicism at a time when propaganda was a necessary tool in helping to spread the cause was perceived to be a major liability. He never imagined that his life would be subject to danger in the hands of the peasants who were his people, he only worried about the Japanese discovering their activities and torturing them all. So when a young comrade who he recognized as an emerging arm-waving leader approached him on a desolate corner on his way home from scavenging food for his family and accused him of being a traitor and a Japanese spy – for not fully embracing their saving grace of sweet smelling communism – he was so shocked that he submitted to his fighting instinct and lunged at his accuser with his fists.

He had not realized his own strength. One blow to the head and the raving communist was out cold. The soon-to-be colonel looked around and quickly fled the area, feeling for the first time the rush of having inflicted pain, which was a strangely exhilarating experience for him, at once cathartic and empowering. It gave him an odd satisfaction to put up a concrete barrier to that detested display of emotions expressed by the unconscious communist and his comrades.

Im In Won quickly fled to his house, dodging both the Japanese police and the locals who indulged in the sweet wafts of ideology behind closed doors and when the time was safe. It wasn't until later that night when his mother entered the house clutching onto her chest that he learned the full scope of his actions. She moaned about how they had taken away Comrade Suh, their last hope of seeing their movement into fruition, another young man whisked away by the Japanese. The locals had discovered the bruised face of the young man who lay unconscious, and soon he

147

was surrounded by sympathizers before the military police arrived, demanding explanations. Everyone started speaking at once and by the time the subject in question had opened his eyes, everyone had been ID'd, questioned, and searched. The authorities also discovered a tiny shred of paper in the emerging leader's pocket with a code that the Japanese could not decipher. When they realized the young man was on their list of civilians held in suspicion of subversive activity, this only strengthened the policemen's resolve and they took in everyone who had been at the scene. Though families of those who were apprehended desperately sought to get answers, the military police refused to release any information.

Im grew very concerned, he knew that his name might be brought up at some point and he realized that he must act fast before either the local people or the authorities got to him. He used the pretext he had not acted on but only talked about for the past few years, that he needed to look elsewhere for jobs and would send money and call for his family once he could find a stable situation. After all, it was his duty as an oldest son. Im declared his intentions to his mother, saying he was going to take a brief journey the next morning to seek work, but that he would return in less than a week.

It was the last time he ever saw his family again.

The next morning, he burned all of his identification papers into a white ash and went by the name only his family called him by and only they knew; he then ventured south primarily as a fugitive, secondarily to seek his destiny in life. When he finally reached Gyeungsong, it did not take long for someone to recognize his military prowess by the stony look of his eyes and he was soon shipped to China to fight on behalf of the emperor of Japan. He flourished in the military and was lauded by his Japanese superiors for his deft ability to wipe out leftist agitators and the nationalists who despised him more than they did their oppressors. He took all of their lives with equal satisfaction, but soon learned that the military was not only about killing. Japan had overestimated their strength in defeating the Allies and it became evident to the colonel, given his *privileged knowledge in the military, that he was on the losing side of what could be a very precarious situation.*

Not a moment too soon, he forfeited the arms of the Japanese emperor and sought shelter in the very nationalist movement he had participated in quelling. While his counterparts who occupied a vast network of exiles – mostly in the United States – were wary of his intentions, their need for military acumen and his impressive credentials of defeating the growing communist movement, overrode their suspicions of him. He soon proved his loyalty to the key figures in the organization by using his military skills as currency. It wasn't long before they forgot about his ignominious stint with the Japanese and forgave him as yet another victim of Power's indiscriminate force.

When the tenacious Japanese military was finally defeated by the Allied troops and retreated back to their island 90 miles away, madness subsumed the peninsula once again, and an ominous demarcation along the 38th parallel severed the colonel's hopes of ever seeing his family again, the one source of truth in his life. Everything in his life since he had turned his back on that arid land had been of his own creation.

This was how Yeon's father found his future son-in-law: devoid of a past, his skin a leathery and impenetrable hide, and decorated with medals of patriotism and hope. He was a perfect solution to Yeon's father's uncertain political future. His daughter however, had not wanted to marry any more than she had wanted to be a pharmacist, though she continued to excel in her chemistry and science courses which helped to mask the secret she kept hidden deep within the confines of her isolated heart.

The only other person in the world with whom she shared her secret, indeed, the only other breathing being except for the heavens itself, knew that the cursed day was encroaching when he would have to see the angel of his existence wed to a man other than himself. They had prepared for that moment ever since their love affair erupted less than two years earlier. He worked in the stables of her father's estate, preparing her horse exactly to her liking for it was from on top of the horse where she sought solace in the animal's untamed spirit and its fierce gallop; from where she could see the earth rippling past her and feel the wind slashing through her hair; where for one small moment she could feel free and imagine she was not chained to the expectations of her parents, society, the world at all, but actually immersed into her own life with all its torrent and fire.

They exchanged nothing more than furtive glances and blind courtesies expected of a young woman and a man of his social class of the time, or any man for that matter. The striking good looks of the boy, covered by the dirt of hard work and peasant attire, would have been enough for any attentive mother to keep him as far away from her daughter as possible, but Yeon's mother was far too busy coddling her sons to know that her daughter was even interested in horses or that she rode as frequently as she did.

For years the two lovers carried on in this way, until the furtive glances turned into bold stares and they looked into each other's eyes and saw themselves in the other's reflection. They looked and said nothing for another couple years, carrying on a dialogue in silence of all they wanted from each other and wondering whether their lives would allow them to succumb to that cosmic force that held their gaze longer and longer and compelled their silent dialogue to explore every thought that had crossed their minds; every dream they entertained within the confines of their existence; every passion that they guarded exclusively for the other; until the day came when Yeon chose not to mount the horse that her secret lover brought to her in reverence.

Instead they stared into each other's eyes until the sun had descended over the horizon and without saying anything, their lips embraced for the first time. Yeon found that she no longer had to ride atop that regal stallion that allowed her soul to roam, for she had gone on the most gilded journeys, traversed the highest mountains, soared to heights far above her temporal existence, and experienced the most ardent and colorful adventures in the eyes of the stable boy. By the time their love affair officially commenced with the seal of their two lips, they had already journeyed to the ends of the earth together and seen far more of the secrets of the universe than some couples who traveled in concert even to the gates of death ever do.

Though they were both ready to die for each other right then and there, it was the young man that convinced his breathing angel that his love was timeless, and that while he was only a useless peasant boy with nothing in the world to lose, she could actually accomplish something with her existence, and live a life he could only dream of providing for her, and that she was more value to him in life rather than death. In this way, the love-struck young man convinced his lover to live, to follow the path laid out for her and persuaded her that the heavens were generous and that they would find themselves together again. He had been so consumed with convincing her of this, in keeping her alive, that he never could brace himself for the tremendous grief that crashed into him like a tsunami when her parents hastily swept her into the arms of the leather-faced colonel while everyone shook their heads in reaction, saying she was far too beautiful to be sold to that symbol of US-sown democracy, purely for her father's political gain.

The wedding had actually backfired on Yeon's father, who the public viewed as just like the other politicians: power-hungry, opportunistic, willing to do anything to advance their own status. And while the concerned politician paced inside the house wondering how to salvage his career, his wife felt vindicated that like she had always intuited, her daughter was even more useless than she could ever have imagined.

Unbeknownst to the politician and his wife, the thunderstorm outside of their home was not a result of high pressure in the atmosphere, but aftershocks of the tremendous heartbreak of their peasant stable boy. The lovers had vowed to see each other no matter the circumstance, but once Yeon entered into her new role and became pregnant almost immediately, she knew she could only see the other half of her heart in heaven. She was filled with pride and too ashamed to see him while she carried her husband's child in her womb, a child that belonged to a stranger and not the love of her life.

Though the colonel worshipped the very ground his beautiful wife traversed, he had killed too many men in his life to ever appreciate the discreet whispers of love and the subtle nuances of the heart. He instead treated her like a doll in his awkward and brutish manner, leaving her expensive jewelry in her jewelry box, never giving her gifts directly but only through servants, and making love to her as if she was not alive which he did frequently and savagely. It was this, combined with both of their ripe fertility that left Yeon with three children before she could even realize what had happened. She had not seen nor heard from her lover since her wedding day but talked to him only in hushed whispers inside her heart. Yeon reverted back to the days of their silent dialogues and whenever she could, nursed a spare moment to speak to him in this unearthly manner. He responded. With words coated in his own blood-soaked tears, he told her how much he missed her, how he longed to see her, how he wished that the gates of heaven would open up for them so they could resume their ethereal journey into the stars.

Yeon considered her lover's yearning and knew she shared in his wish. She cursed herself for following through with the wedding and doing what was expected of her as she always did. She continued to have children until she produced an heir after her third try. She had succeeded even in giving birth to a son. There was nothing more she could offer to this unjust world. Yeon looked at her two daughters and baby son and wondered what her life had become. She loved her children. Aside from the silent dialogue in her heart they were the one pure thing in her life. Her father's political career was in shambles and her parents' finances were depleted after the countless wons they poured into advancing his career.

Even her father who had been the only one of the two who paid her any attention, looked at her as if she had committed the ultimate betrayal. He learned through her the danger of having daughters, when they reach a certain age and become marriageable, they simply fade away.

Yeon thought to herself as she did countless times, that if she disappeared from the world her parents would neither notice nor care. Her siblings would feel sad, she thought. She was, after all, the oldest and they looked up to her, but they too would soon get over their heartache once the demands of life gripped them. But her children? What would become of her children? She vowed never to be like her own mother and she treated them all equitably and distributed her forlorn attentions to them as best as her broken heart would allow. But even her children, as much as she loved them, could not replace her diminished will to live. She decided that if she were to chase after her love, she would have to do so soon. Her children were at that age when they would have virtually no memory of her, no recollection of her having existed. She thought this would be better for everyone and would ease the pain of the children for whom her own mother and husband would surely find a replacement. The only one she worried about was the oldest, who was going on four and who shared the same pensive, thoughtful disposition of her mother as well as her premature wisdom. Yeon realized that more was required with this child, so when the time was right, she took her aside after she laid her younger two children to sleep.

"Wansonah," she whispered, stroking her first-born's hair, "one thing you must always remember in life is how much your mother loves you. Every decision you make, every choice you face you must make with the conviction that your mother loves you."

The mournful round brown eyes looked up at her. "Why are you saying this o-ma? Where are you going?"

"I don't know where I'm going my love, but no matter where I am I will always be inside your heart. You must know this always. Promise me that you will never forget how much I love you."

The telepathic toddler nodded her head in knowing resignation, "I promise o-ma."

"Promise me that you will only make decisions based on this fact. A woman's success depends on her mother's love."

"I promise omonee."

After that conversation, Yeon felt that there was nothing left to do but to make her arrangements for her exit from this world. She summoned her lover through the cosmic forces of the universe, and together they planned to meet again with the new moon on the other side of existence. She convinced him that this was the only way out, and he agreed with her after the profound suffering he had endured for the past four years without her. She put her excellent training in pharmaceuticals into good use and after acquiring various powders and inhalants from different providers so nothing could be traced to one source, she began mixing, crushing, and stirring a compound in her own bathroom until she had produced the perfect amount of the deadliest dose of poison that was tasteless, scentless, and as of the science of the times, impossible to trace. She then asked the blacksmith to make the finest horseshoe for her, keeping one end of it hollow. Like most people she dealt with who were captivated by her grace and beauty, he asked no questions but set to make a sturdy horseshoe with one hollow end. When the piece of art was delivered to her she inserted the second vile of her poison into it and summoned a young servant girl to deliver the horseshoe to the young man at the stable who worked at her parents' estate. Yeon did not need to tell the little girl not to say anything, everyone who interacted with Yeon treasured those moments with her within the secrets of their own sacred memories.

The day before the new moon, he confirmed through their silent language of love, that he had received her beautiful package and would see her very soon. The house was a bustle on New Year's Eve. Everyone was preparing for the extravagant gala she and the colonel were hosting as a final push for her father's waning career. It was a very important evening for her parents, all the key figures would be attending, and she volunteered to host it knowing how much it meant to both of them. It was their last chance in salvaging her father's future. Knowing the financial strain her parents were under, she organized every piece of jewelry she accumulated throughout the years, for her husband bought her only the most exquisite pieces. She carefully laid them in her jewelry box to have ready to give to her father at precisely 11:37pm. Yeon then got ready for the party, putting on her finest gown and wrapping a string of pearls around her neck.

The gala was the most coveted event of the season. Friends and political enemies dressed in their finest stood impressed by the incredible evening the hosts had prepared. Everyone's eye was on the host's gorgeous daughter, who acted as the perfect hostess and captivated her father's most stubborn opposition with her elegant charm and intelligent wit. The politician's enemies would have forgiven him anything if they could get just one moment with his daughter. At around 11:30pm Yeon approached her father and discreetly informed him that she was putting her two older children to bed, she then turned to the men he was speaking with and said, "Excuse me gentleman, my daughters adore their grandfather and insist on saying 'goodnight' to him, I will return him to you right away."

She then led him to her bedroom and took the jewelry box out and handed it to him with both hands.

"Aboji, please take this as a small gesture from my husband and me as we wish we had much more to offer you. It is our small contribution to your campaign."

Her father's pride a little bruised, insisted on handing the box back to his daughter who refused to take it. "Please father, it is nothing. I do not need these jewels and would like them to go to better use. You could get a good amount from what's in there, enough to tide you over at least."

After some going back and forth, the humbled father finally agreed, grateful for the donation. Yeon then shooed him back to the party as she really was about to tuck her two children into bed. The servants who had been watching them saw their lady and indicated to her that the children had already fallen asleep. She asked for a moment with them alone and gave each of her children final kisses while they ventured throughout their world of dreams.

Yeon took off her string of pearls and laid them in the hand of her oldest daughter. Then she turned around and made the lugubrious steps back to the bedroom. She indicated to one of the servants that she had a headache and would like to be left alone and asked them to tell the guests, if anyone inquired, that she would be returning to the party shortly. The gala was in full swing however, and everyone was long under the influence of the bottles of liquor and had very few cares in the world. They eagerly awaited the New Year which was minutes away.

Yeon pulled out the vial of poison that she had tucked inside her pantyhose and lied down on the bed. When the clock struck 11:57pm she swallowed the contents of the vial and closed her eyes. It would not take long for the concoction to take effect. Less than a mile away, the stable boy, now a young man, did the same, gripping a horseshoe in his left hand. By 12:01am, both of their hearts had come to a complete stop.

They slipped into death, just as they had lived their lives, quietly and unnoticed, like two specters sweeping in and out between the crevices of life. Yet another pair of casualties of love. They joined others like them on the other side of existence: other souls who lacked the will to continue with the charades life had required of them, others who could not break free from the agonizing imprisonment of forbidden love. The string of pearls melted in the palm of Yeon's sleeping daughter's hand and when she awoke the next morning, no one could explain the sparkling powder that coated her hand like a glove. Inside her hand and inside her heart were the remnants of crushed pearls and the bleeding memory of her mother telling her that she is loved. She vowed to her mother that she would never forget that moment and all her life she never did, trailing the path behind her with the shimmering dust from the palm of her hand.

But suicide was not as easy to forgive. As one of few people who knew the truth, including her grandparents, her father, and her new stepmother, all of whom swiftly swept the whole affair under the rug, Wanso's already solemn disposition, took on a morose hue, and when she grew into an adult, people wondered what it would take to coax a smile from the sober-faced woman. But smiles were a luxury she could not afford. She had too many secrets wrapped up inside her broken heart to concern herself with such displays of emotion. Instead, Wanso did everything she could to substitute a love toward her younger sister and brother that her own mother could never give to any of them. Yeon's oldest daughter sought to protect all the moments of purity she shared with her siblings and to do her best against life's capricious and earth-shattering travails.

What she learned from suicide was that nothing in life is sacred. What she learned from living was that everything is.

PART III: DIVISION

Space and time collide -
the pressurized tomb
of vaulted memory.
We were one
And now we're scattered
among the ash and star dust.

Enter the Americans

1948

The beauty of the land that April was deceiving. The blinding yellows of forsythia carved paths into the landscape while bursts of azaleas erupted onto the scene like passion. Snow glistened from the rugged mountaintops and hearkened toward the heavens for mercy.

Sa Mi walked along the dirt road clutching two-year-old Young to her breast as seven-year-old Hyun-jin, and four-year-old Kyu-jin, walked on either side of her. Sa Mi stared down at the road which was covered with cherry blossoms. Had she looked up, she would have noticed the blossoms fluttering off the trees and onto their shoulders and hair like a spring snow.

But Sa Mi did not dare to look up. After all, the Americans were in town. With their large bodies, round eyes, and heavy army boots, they intimidated Sa Mi more than the Japanese ever did. She had heard stories about the GIs and what they did to young women like her, treating them all like the girls that worked the military bases for a shred of hope and a green card. So as Sa Mi walked down the road, she kept her children close by and minded her own business.

Sa Mi did not know whether to feel relief or fear when the American soldiers first arrived. Though they were known to be the liberators – the ones that finally stopped Japan before she encroached upon the entire eastern hemisphere – Sa Mi felt uneasy by their entitled presence. Some of the people resented the Americans who sauntered onto the peninsula trampling over everything with their colossal army boots and mistaking the Koreans for their war enemies, the Japanese. Others heralded them as heroes.

Things had been chaotic since Japan had surrendered. The Soviets came down from the North while the Americans occupied the South, announcing that the country would operate under two different governments separated by the 38th parallel. Friends of Sa Mi who had been visiting the Cholla-do province in the South to see family, immediately retreated back to their homes in the north, promising to return once their country was back in order.

Sa Mi could not understand what was happening to her life and to her country. She remembered her days of longing for her husband, her moments of song, and her accurate predictions of the harvest which impressed her father-in-law so much. She was surrounded by servants in those days and decorated with finery, but now, almost overnight, she and her family were left with nothing. She had never ceased to be lonely even in her days of abundance. But now her children had nothing to eat and they were all relegated to a two-room dwelling just a mile down from where their estate used to be. It was as if everything had been a dream, so unreal it seemed. If her husband was not sitting at home in the same catatonic state he had been in for weeks, she would resent him and his gambling ways like any wife would.

Instead, she pitied him. The secret worship she observed for him as a young bride could not be fully extinguished. She was not alone in her admiration for her ruined husband. People were easy to forgive Sun his vices in light of his magnetic charm and lightening wit. But even they didn't have to live with the consequences of such qualities. Charisma was of little use when it came to raising a family and surviving the financial and political turmoil that besieged them. Still, Sa Mi forgave Sun for what he was as he was not much different from her in this regard. They were both products of a time long forgotten, thrust into a time forever to be remembered.

And they had mouths to feed. Plenty of them. Fortunately, the three oldest children were married, struggling as well with the chaos of the times, but nowhere near the desperation that their parents had reached. They rarely heard from Soonjin, who still carried the bitter fruit of never having known her birth mother and the circumstances surrounding her entry into the world. Sa Mi and Sun knew Soonjin lived in the capital Geyoungsong, which was now renamed Seoul under the provisional government, but of Soonjin's daily existence and the trials and celebrations of her life, they knew nothing.

Sa Mi and Sun sent their next two sons to live in Seoul with their oldest son Bong-jin and his wife so that Jong-jin and Yu-jin might finish school and receive some regularity of meals. The older of the two sons, Jong-jin, put his brilliant mind to good use by taking on as many tutoring pupils as he could manage to contribute to the cost of the family meals, but according to their sister-in-law it was never enough.

The younger of the two, Yu-jin, woke up one day to an "iridescent dream" (his words) which compelled him to shave his head and abstain from drink, women, and food so he might join the venerable monks in the mountains. Jong-jin, who tolerated the slights he received from the sons of the rich families he tutored in order to keep them both afloat, met Yu-jin's aspirations with sheer disgust, for any talk of religion nauseated him. The two brothers could not have been more different and had they not shared the same blood, one would question whether their paths in life would have ever crossed. The only thing they had in common was their desire to leave their brother and sister-in-law's home.

The arguing and the mere presence of her husband's family added to their sister-in-law's aggravations. There was no end to Bong-jin's wife's complaints about her husband and his *good-for-nothing family* which she frequently and liberally referred to with contempt. The two houseguests were joined in their sympathy for their older brother whom they did not blame when he came home with alcohol on his breath and empty pockets. In spite of their sympathies for the fate of their oldest brother, it wasn't long before Jong-jin began putting away some money to rent a room for him and his younger brother, despite Yu-jin's insistence to join the monastery. Their impending departure however, did not quell their sister-in-law's vocal chords or her overall disdain for her husband and his entire family.

Sa Mi sent Dong-jin, their next oldest son, to live with her daughter, Mijin, whose first year of marriage had not turned out to be the honeymoon that everyone, including the young couple, had expected. Soon after the wedding, the young bride's father-in-law took a much younger wife of his own and left his bitter ex-wife to the care and support of his son. The handsome English teacher and his new bride were now responsible for the jilted woman. With her son as the sole lifeboat of her existence, she clung to him and unleashed her anger at her spoiled, beautiful daughter-in-law, confusing her likeness with the tramp that had stolen her husband. Now that her ex-husband was spending all of his earnings on his new wife, money became scarce, which sent the bitter mother-in-law into a panic. She was tolerable when she was comforted by the excesses of her husband's money, but without it, she turned into an absolute monster.

Scarcity only further fueled the resentment she had toward her daughter-in-law Mijin, as she saw her son spending his earnings on her and indulging her fancies while she was left with nothing. When the bitter old woman finally heard about the ill fortune that had befallen her daughter-in-law's parents, she grew even more livid and insatiable, feeling that she had been duped into marrying her fine son off to a daughter of paupers. And when

Mijin's younger brother came to live with them, it was enough for the mother-in-law to send both the boy and his sister packing, far away from her precious son.

With her older children's domestic lives as tenuous and chaotic as their country's uncertain future, Sa Mi walked along the street with her three youngest children, the babes that she could not afford to feed.

Hyun was her seven-year-old gem who refused to suckle at her breast one frigid day in December and who didn't seem to shake the coldness of his demeanor ever since. He was an exceedingly studious and intelligent child who won his parents' affections early on and his refusal to reciprocate such affections only made his parents vie for them more. Like for many talented children, Hyun's intellect became his crutch throughout the trying times of his life and buried access to the mysteries locked away in his heart. Hyun relied on the devices of his head: his ability to think, to calculate and to analyze; and he favored the likes of his brain far more than that turbulent, unreliable, unpredictable, fickle heart of his.

If Hyun was their gem, his curly haired younger sister was the nuisance of a pebble in their parents' shoes. Sun had cursed her curly hair at the time of her birth which marked the beginning of his tragic luck and the poor child had never recovered. To add to this injury of birthright, Kyu-jin demanded to be the center of attention with her cutesy ways and witty remarks. Sun, who was accustomed to the solemn disposition of his eldest, illegitimate daughter, and the gentle, reserved disposition of his legitimate one, was troubled by the brashness of this daughter. Combined with his fragile state and Sa Mi's tendency to submit to her husband's lead, Kyu-jin became blameworthy of everything bad that came their way. Together, the couple kept their attentions toward the adorable girl reserved for scoldings.

Sometime ago in her foggy past, Sa Mi had criticized her sister-in-law for her uneven attentions toward her children, and more specifically, the injustice with which she treated her oldest daughter. Sa Mi had long forgotten the righteousness that she had asserted with her sister-in-law but fell comfortably into her own habits of favoritism among the children she birthed.

The babe that Sa Mi held in her arms however was a solemn little thing and both she and her husband were rather intimidated by the child in the same way they were by their gem of a son. This babe did not cry but on rare occasions and with her wet round eyes, explored the world around her in a knowing silence. When she looked up at her parents she did so with empathy, as if she knew she had been born into hard times. Out of all her children, Sa Mi's heart went out to this child who was inadequately nourished for there were no more wet nurses around and Sa Mi herself did not have a proper diet to produce more than watery drops of milk. When she could no longer summon a drop of milk from her breast, Sa Mi would wet the sash of her *hanbok* and have the baby suckle on it so at the very least, she could wet the child's mouth.

Understanding that life had not much to offer her while she was awake, little Young spared everyone the pain of feedings by sleeping all hours of the day and night. This was her present state when her mother carried her in her arms and walked along the unpaved road with her other two children on either side.

"*Omonee*, where are we going?" inquired little Kyu-jin, her full cheeks surrounded by curls.

"Quiet," sighed Sa Mi in irritation, "didn't I tell you not to ask such questions to adults and to not speak unless you're spoken to?"

"How long will we be gone?" followed up Hyun in an ominous tone, neither heeding nor acknowledging his mother's words.

To her prized son she simply stammered, "Not long. Just until your father and I are able to straighten out some matters." After a few beats Sa Mi added, "You will receive three square meals a day where we're going. And there will be other children to play with as well."

"Other children?!" Kyu-jin asked excitedly while her older brother, who was not much of a social animal, simply grunted.

"Yes, that's right," Sa Mi replied, swallowing back the lump in her throat.

When they reached the brown wooden building at the bottom of the hill, shouts of children could be heard and the little bodies that were responsible for all the noises could be seen running around the premises as three women supervised the disorder.

Hyun couldn't believe his eyes. *This* was where his mother was going to leave him and his sisters?! But all the children were so *dirty* in their dingy clothes and he abhorred the hungry look in their eyes as they stopped to stare at them. Had his parents gone mad?! He would rather starve than to stay there! He was so in shock that he could not find the words to say anything to his mother. Instead, as she spoke with one of the women, he simply narrowed his eyes toward Sa Mi to display his dissatisfaction, but she refused to look directly at him.

"These are my three," Sa Mi indicated to the woman. "Please, you must help, I have not a grain of rice to feed them, and this one," looking down at her bundle, "I fear she needs something in her belly, please, even a little *jook* and she is satisfied, she really is..."

"I'm sorry *ajumma*, but the baby is too young, we don't have the..."

"Please," interrupted Sa Mi, "you must help me, she is an angel and all she does is sleep, just feed her some porridge while I am gone and I'll be back for her, for all of them, soon. My husband and I are going through hard times."

Knowing all too well about the hard times to which Sa Mi referred, as she was not the first mother to come and leave her children at the orphanage until times got better, the woman reluctantly agreed.

"This here is Hyun," Sa Mi continued, still avoiding her son's piercing eyes, "he is absolutely brilliant and loves school. These are his books," handing Hyun his bag, "and he spends his time studying when he's not in school. You'll hardly notice him. And over here is Kyu-jin," but when Sa Mi turned to her other side she noticed her daughter was busy already talking to the other children. How out of place she looked in her fine silk *hanbok*, while all the children eyed her with curiosity. "Well, that is her anyway," Sa Mi indicated with a wave of her hand.

"And when will you return for them?" asked the lady skeptically, knowing in her heart that some mothers never return.

"In just a few weeks, as soon as my husband straightens out his affairs," Sa Mi replied.

"I will need you to check back in a week for the little one, I'm not sure we can hold her any longer than that," then to be sure that Sa Mi understood the seriousness of her concerns and so she would stay true to her word, "I'm afraid that if she is not picked up in a week, there are plenty of white Christian missionaries who love Asian babies, surely they will see fit to take her on the spot. Now that the whites rule our land, I am powerless to them."

Horrified by the woman's story Sa Mi nodded her head furiously and told her that she would check on the children in less than a week's time. She kissed the still sleeping baby gently on the forehead and handed her to the social worker. She then knelt down to Hyun and, avoiding his eyes and focusing instead on his meticulously shined shoes, she told him to be good and to watch over his younger sisters. Hyun said not a word, but the scowl he wore on his face spoke volumes. Her curly-haired daughter ran to her and hugged her realizing that Sa Mi was now leaving. Sa Mi squeezed her, thanked the lady who had inherited yet more children for the Lord's work, and turned towards home, her son's eyes burning into her back until she was no longer visible.

As she walked toward home she thought neither of the US servicemen who passed by her, nor about anything else but the look on her son's face as she left her children behind. Unable to fathom their wretched and destitute state, and as sole proof of her journey, Sa Mi left behind a muddy trail of tears.

Hyun-jin

Filial piety was not a virtue he could claim. A bitter seed was planted in his heart the day his mother turned around and left him and his sisters in the orphanage. Hyun had watched Sa Mi's silhouette fading over the horizon until she disappeared into the immense sky and he swore that forgiveness for such an affront would be impossible in his lifetime. The first thing he did every morning was to look out the window in the direction where she had faded away to see whether she would return, but he only saw dust up-ended from the American tanks and a shadow of what was to come.

Though he was not alone (there were other children whose mothers also left them there in hope of better care), Hyun only paid attention to those children whose mothers came every day to check on their well-being. The tragic look of love on their faces and their sweet motherly scent placed such a longing in his little heart that the more he saw those mothers visiting their children, the more he resented his own mother. When Sa Mi finally did return as she had promised in less than a week's time, Hyun looked but could not find that tragic look on his mother's face. Her face was too flawless to bear pain and her creamy complexion hid nothing. Aside from appearing perhaps tired and devoid of answers, she lacked the messy, tragic dispositions of the other mothers whose eyes said everything. Even in her torn and degraded state, Sa Mi was meticulously groomed and still looked like a wealthy landlord's wife. In Hyun's mind, his mother was of little use. Stoicism should be reserved only for men. Women who attempted this ideal, like his own mother, appeared to him to be cold and distant; he wanted a mother who would bleed for him.

Sa Mi returned at just the right time. Hyun had noticed that his baby sister had not taken the departure of their mother well either. Soon after Sa Mi left, Young awoke from her peaceful slumber and looked onto the world in fearful confusion and not the knowing silence that her mother had always observed in her. The women at the orphanage tried in vain to feed her and the child refused even water. She began to appear sickly and pale and as the nurse on staff tried helplessly to keep her from dehydration, everyone looked on in worry and horror. Had Sa Mi arrived even a day later, the circumstances could have become dire. And at the first sight of her poor babe, Sa Mi had to keep herself from fainting. Immediately, her maternal instincts surfaced and the need to save her baby caused milk to flow to her breast.

Upon recognition of her mother, the baby abandoned her look of fear and desperately suckled. Everyone breathed a sigh of relief and even Sa Mi could not contain her overwhelming emotion which culminated in a tear at the corner of her eye. She cradled and nursed her babe and Hyun thought for sure that she would take them all back with her, this time for good. Instead, after hearing what a model child her son was and how her daughter was faring so well among the other children, Sa Mi brushed her hand against his cheek, which he instinctively stiffened against, and thanked him for being such a good boy. She then proceeded to tell him that she would need him to continue to stay at the orphanage just awhile longer and promised that she would come back for him. In the meantime, she would take his baby sister with her.

Hyun stared back at the strange woman before him but said not a word. Sa Mi took his silence for acquiescence and praised him again for his model behavior. Then, bundling up her sick babe she thanked the women at the orphanage and walked back down the same dirt road that Hyun awoke to stare at every morning. This time he did not watch her as she faded into the dust but turned his own back before she disappeared. It was his way of asserting his own devices. Hyun realized that day that he was capable of turning his back on others. If he always turned his back first, he would never have to be a victim again.

Meanwhile, Sa Mi made her way back up the dusty road with her babe held securely in her arms. She left yet another trail of tears and wondered to herself when the madness that had compelled her to do the unthinkable would finally end. The signs were foreboding. All over the Cholla-do province there were violent uprisings and bloodshed. There were also leftist guerrillas hiding in the mountains just waiting to attack members of the old aristocracy like she and her husband. The level of poverty to which they had been reduced didn't matter. All the remnants of the former elite were cast in the same light. It didn't help that her brother-in-law was a politician in their province and was favored by the right to represent his constituency. The guerrillas were thirsty for him and any of his relatives. Sa Mi's brother-in-law and his wife were well aware of the seriousness of Sa Mi and Sun's plight but treated it less with sympathy and more with filial shame. The extension of a helping hand was absolutely out of the question. They had their own issues to deal with and running a campaign during such a bloody time in their country's history was not an easy feat. They needed all of their resources in order to seal Sa Mi's brother-in-law's fate in history.

Just months before South Korea's first election, Sa Mi's brother-in-law hosted a lavish party in their daughter's home. Sa Mi and Sun were not invited. It wasn't until weeks later that they learned that their niece, Yeon, who was at one time inseparable from their own daughter Mijin, had died at that party. Her sister-in-law never spoke a word about it to Sa Mi. With their political connections, they were even able to keep it out of the newspapers. Sa Mi happened to have caught wind of the rumors that were circulating, and though there were many different versions, for no one was sure what the cause of death was, Sa Mi had convinced herself that forbidden love was the culprit. It gave her some peace to believe that her niece's exit from the world was not one cast in misery, but an act of romantic desperation. This made the tragedy somewhat more bearable and others around the lonely girl – including Sa Mi – less culpable.

It was her daughter that called to tell Sa Mi that her other cousin, the deceased's younger sister, was quickly and quietly wed to her widowed brother-in-law, as if nothing had happened. It was almost as if their eldest daughter had never existed. Sa Mi reflected on how weddings often followed funerals. She recalled her own fate and how she had not even begun grieving her own mother's death before her sisters had tried to marry her off. But that seemed so long ago, and there was too much to deal with in the present to think about the past.

Hunger was what haunted every minute of every day.

She tried not to concern herself with her own hunger as she had little ones to worry about, and though she knew it seemed cruel to leave them at that orphanage, she couldn't conceive of any other way. Their hunger and her own hunger collided into a giant mass that followed her everywhere she went like an ominous shadow. To be alone with your hunger is a loneliness of the worst kind and at least there at the orphanage her children would receive rations of grain. Of course, it wasn't much either but it was more than she could provide. Though money had become completely devalued into useless scraps of paper, loan sharks continued to demand their share and when they had it, Sa Mi and her husband would helplessly give up the small portions of grain they had accumulated from the generosity of former tenants. Sa Mi refused to visit her children unless she could bring them something to satiate the cruel beast that lurked in their stomachs, so when she was left empty-handed again, Sa Mi decided she would wait until next time, when she would have something to offer. She never imagined that she had anything more to offer them, for love never kept anyone from dying of hunger. She felt like a failure of the worst kind, but who knew how quickly things could just disappear?

Her husband appeared to be even worse off than she. He walked around the streets of their village in a dazed stupor, trying to maintain his sense of dignity in the presence of his fellow villagers, while seeking some way out of the mess he had a hand in creating.

There were times when it was too dangerous to walk outside. One had to negotiate the political rallies which inevitably led to violence, as well as the mobs of people that surrounded the communist organizers when they distributed grain in exchange for loyalties. When Sun read the temptation on his wife's face to retrieve some grain herself, he looked fiercely into her eyes to dissuade her motherly instinct. And when he felt like the look alone was not enough, he said simply, "You will get us all killed." He knew there was nothing more dangerous than a people with hunger in their bellies and freedom on their minds. The tension in the air in his country only showed signs of getting worse.

Sa Mi listened to her husband, though it pained her to do so as she could think of nothing more foolish than to pass up food in times of such scarcity. As she walked down the main road of her town holding her babe in her arms, she was approached by a merchant's wife, who had also experienced ill luck, and with whom Sa Mi had shared several exchanges when she used to buy beautiful textiles from her.

"*Eonni, eonni!*" she cried, knowing that Sa Mi was upon hard times. Holding a sack of rice, she waved it in front of her face saying, "The Reds have bestowed their generosity once again!

They do more for us than these Yankees who stand by as our children starve. Go quick! They are still there, you can still fill your sack of rice!" she said excitedly, feeling she was fulfilling her neighborly duties.

Sa Mi acknowledged the younger woman with a nod of her head then looked down at her pale, undernourished child who now that she was in her mother's arms, slept peacefully despite her hunger. Sa Mi then looked up again at the woman who stood before her waving her bag of rice. She paused, bowed her head again and said, "I'm sorry but I cannot accept charity for such causes." Not knowing what else to do, Sa Mi then continued walking with her babe bundled up in her arms.

The merchant's wife stood in the road stunned, feeling as she had just been slapped. There was truth to what the Reds said after all, the old guard of the elite were truly worth nothing. Did Sa Mi honestly think that she was better than her just because she was a landlord's wife (who, by the way, was no longer a landlord anyway), and she, nothing more than a lowly merchant? So Sa Mi was too good to accept handouts even though her baby wore the look of death? Unbelieving, the insulted woman spat into the ground and continued to walk in the direction of her own home. There was change in the air and this merchant's wife welcomed it. There was nothing that irritated her more than the sheer stupidity and disconnect with reality that those like Sa Mi possessed. "Let them all starve," she thought to herself, "surely they have been responsible for the hunger of others all these years."

When Sa Mi reached the humility of their new home, she called out in vain for her husband. She then unwrapped her baby girl and noticed that her husband had left a handful of barley on a sheet of rice paper. Sa Mi breathed a sigh of relief and boiled the barley to make porridge for her hungry babe. Little did she know that she had just missed her husband. Sun had left the house in a hurry right before she arrived. Apparently, an old friend from the past had showed up again in Damyang. The journalist who had been carted away years ago was alive after all.

Childong Returns

S un drummed his fingertips on the surface of the wooden table. Poetry escaped him and he could not find the words nor begin to describe the demons that had come to corrupt his soul. There was an ugliness that surrounded him, a disquietude that continued to ripple from every direction, charging through the center of his soul to implode. The tea at the *tabang* was watered down and cold, but the owner of the tea house had extended it to him graciously saying it was "on the house" for Yi *saboneem*. It was the owner's way of allowing the fallen landlord to save face for they both knew that Sun had nothing to offer.

Sun had been approached by a young boy earlier in the day. He thought for sure it was an orphan begging for food. Instead, the young boy bowed to him and said he was there to deliver a message.

"An old friend has asked to meet with you *saboneem*. He has just come to town and will only be here for this day. He asked that you meet him at the same place you have always met at around two in the afternoon. He wanted me to tell you not to worry, that the police would not recognize him this time."

Sun started at the young boy's last line. He could only be talking about one person. Though he had not given up complete hope, Sun assumed that his childhood friend had been imprisoned and even killed by the Japanese. He kept his ears open after the end of the occupation, but this was the first that he had heard anything about Childong. He stood there staring at the boy's half-moon pendant hanging from his neck, before he responded hastily, "Yes, yes of course, let him know I'll see him later today...at our regular meeting spot."

"*Nae saboneem*," the boy bowed politely. Sun searched his pockets for anything to give to the young boy for his troubles, but both his pouch and pockets were empty save for the broken chain to his gold pocket watch that he had long since pawned without the chain. He held onto the chain in hopes of one day getting the watch back or buying a new one, and it lied at the bottom of his barren money pouch, reminding him of his new-found poverty. On the flat side of the link was engraved the three symbols of his name.

"*Cha*," he said to the boy, "This is all I have. It's pure gold. Though it isn't much, you should be able to get something for yourself with that."

The boy's eyes lit up at the sight of the chain which he received with both hands. As he walked away from Sun the messenger continued bowing his head in gratitude, saying that he would let the mystery man know of Sun's answer right away.

And so, we find Sun, nursing cold tea at the *tabang* where his friend had been carted away years earlier. Though he could only imagine the hard times Childong must have experienced, he wondered if the journalist would even recognize him in his depraved state. He was not his normal self, so much had the depression seized him, deflating him of his dignity. Though Sun still maintained his meticulous appearance there was no hiding the barren look in his eyes. A man devoid of his dignity is barely recognizable.

Sun knew that two of his children were being cared for at the local orphanage for the time being and that his wife had gone to retrieve their youngest baby. He was not ready to accept the reality of what this meant for he could see no way out of the mess that he had created. Several times he sought in vain to contact his oldest son, Bong-jin, whose responsibility it was to look after the family when such misfortune struck, but this son inherited only his father's complacency and charm and seemed to struggle with handling his own wife and home. Bong-jin still roamed around indulging himself without seeking or holding onto any kind of work to help out his family. It was Sun's idea to put his head together with his *changnam* to find some way to save their family from complete ruin, but it was of no use. Behind his son's good looks and charming smile there were only good intentions and broken promises. Bong-jin won the favor of others with his smile and gentle demeanor alone, but to his wife and to his father he was useless. In Sun's eyes, his oldest son would never amount to anything.

Still, he had no other hope during these trying times and when Sun was finally able to reach Bong-jin, his oldest son insisted that his parents come to Seoul for a visit, where surely there must be more opportunities than there were in Damyang. Sun considered this as a last resort and planned to leave with Sa Mi to visit the capital the following week. The futility of trying to find a way out of their mess in their depressed village, which bubbled over with leftist activities, only added to his frustration and anxieties.

As Sun wallowed in his worries and uncertainties, he noticed a man enter the tea house in plain white peasant clothes and a beard. At first, he looked like an elderly *haraboji*, but as Sun took a closer look something rang familiar in the stranger's eyes. With every step the stranger made toward Sun, Sun scrutinized him until the old man walked right up to Sun and said, "Is this how you greet an old friend?"

Sun gasped at the sound of the familiar voice, "Is it really true? Is it really you? How much you've changed!" he declared embracing his childhood friend.

To this the stranger replied, "You don't look so young and vibrant yourself, though the bourgeois attire softens some of the blows," indicating Sun's top hat and aristocratic garb.

"And I see that you're still in hiding," pointing toward his friend's rugged appearance, then motioning his hand for him to take a seat and following suit himself, "My friend, have you not heard that the war is finally over?" The owner's wife eyed the strange man curiously, but quickly placed a cup of tea before him then shuffled away.

Rubbing his beard, the journalist let out a chuckle, "My dear friend, you haven't changed a bit have you? It's no wonder you write such elegant poetry, as detached from reality as you can be." Then, lowering his head and shifting his demeanor, he said, "I hate to break it to you but this is not a time for elegance, there is a new war on the horizon and a new enemy that has usurped our land."

Nodding his head, Sun slowly took a sip of his tea and paused thoughtfully. "I suppose war has become the answer to everything these days. Perhaps we can just kill one another, bomb each other to pieces to eliminate all of our differences at once. Then there will be no more problems to solve."

"This is where we have found ourselves. There are consequences to decades of violence, and it is our turn to fight back."

There was something in his friend's voice that disturbed Sun. The passion he had always known his friend to possess had metamorphosed into something else altogether. There was a glow in his eyes that Sun had seen before in the eyes of the Japanese policeman the same day his friend first disappeared many years ago. It was hard to believe that he found the same disposition in the friend that sat before him. He tried in vain to change the subject, "So, where have you been all of these years? How did you manage?"

As if he didn't hear Sun's question, the ex-journalist looked into Sun's face in silence and asked, "Do you know what it is to suffer?" Without waiting for his friend to answer Childong continued, "Do you know what it is to feel all alone in this world, to feel you have nothing to lose, nothing to hang onto?"

Sun felt a pain in his stomach and managed to say, "I'm sorry, what you must have been through these years...I can't even begin to imagine..."

"The Japanese? Yes. They tortured me, spat on me, tried to break me. But that's not what I'm talking about. I escaped them in my mind long before I escaped physically. They could never touch my spirit."

Sun sat silently, waiting for Childong to continue.

"It's the pain inflicted by my own people that I cannot escape. Do you know that I cannot recall my mother's face, and I have forgotten even the sound of my father's voice? Do you know how useless they were to me after they died? Do you know what it is to be without family in that sacred world we live in of social class and illusions? Growing up, people looked at me like I was no better than an orphan begging on the street. I never wanted to be pitied by anyone. You ask me why I wear this?" he asked, clutching onto to his white peasant garb, "This isn't a costume. This is how I feel at home. I understand the pain of the people. The same people our ancestors stepped on for years."

179

The words were like daggers piercing Sun's soul. He looked straight at the face of the childhood friend that was once so familiar to him, "My father cared for you like a son."

"But I was not his son, I was never his son. I will always be grateful to him for what he did for me, but do you understand that the reason I chose a profession and worked and bled for it was because I didn't have a choice? Everything died with my parents when I was a child and as far as I'm concerned, my family name means nothing. The past is dead."

"Your father was an honorable man."

"My father is dead."

"Our fathers, our ancestors, they never set out to hurt anybody, they would never step on anyone like you say, they inherited the times they lived in...This was just how it was."

"I've bit my tongue for many years, but I have to tell you old friend, you are terribly naïve. You think that just because you can roam around in your own little protected world, idling yourself at the gambling table and writing poetry when the spirit moves you that others live like you? Others suffer while you indulge your every whim. This is how it has always been."

Sun's building anger at the stranger before him caused his voice to lower into a whisper, "And I suppose you have an answer for me. What do you want me to do? Do you know that I have nothing? I've lost *everything*. I haven't even a crumb to feed my own family."

"It doesn't feel good does it?" Then leaning forward again, "I want you to let go of all these illusions you have, to let go of the past and to stop parading around in traditions that have no meaning anymore. I want you to fight for once in your life. To fight for what is right and just."

"And I take it that murder is just to you?"

"I want you to take freedom by whatever means necessary. But I fear you are too far gone, too deeply rapt in your own illusions. I came here to warn you, to shake you out of your slumber and to let you know that this is your chance to awaken yourself."

Sun couldn't believe his ears, "You've come here to *warn* me? What makes you think that I don't know what is happening in our country?"

"Look at you! Just take a look at you and your ridiculous top hat! Look around you! You talk about liberation and all I see are American tanks and people with nothing to eat! This isn't liberation, things are far worse here than they were even under the Japanese."

"And I suppose things are better in the North?"

"Yes!" the glowing eyes declared, "Yes, much better! People are being given rights they never dreamed of. They are letting go of the past, of illusions that don't matter anymore, of ideas that never mattered."

"So, you are choosing one foreign occupier over another. What is so lofty about that?"

"Hmphf," the ex-journalist grunted, "Spoken like a true American imperialist."

"Don't insult me," replied Sun sternly, "believe it or not I only want freedom, just like you. But why more killing?"

"Do you know how many Japanese I killed after I escaped to China? None of those lives equal the pain they inflicted on our people."

"I suppose there will never be an adequate number."

"You say I insult you with my words but answer me one question. How can anyone who truly wants freedom, come out in public and support that tyrannical American agent Syngman Rhee for president?"

"You're referring to my brother?"

"Yes, I am referring to your family, to you, you are one and the same. According to the rules blood is all that matters, though we will be changed soon, I promise."

"He is the most qualified for the job. This country cannot be unified under a Soviet system."

"Do you say that because you fear that *you* will lose out, or do you mean that it is truly what is best for the country?"

"I told you that I have lost everything, there is nothing left for anyone to take away from me."

"Do you know that Syngman Rhee spent more years in the United States than he has in his own country?"

"Like Kim Il Sung has spent most of his years in China?"

"Fighting for *your* freedom!" the ex-journalist replied pounding his fist on the table which caused the owner of the *tabang* to look up. "While Syngman Rhee was rubbing noses with the Americans at Princeton or whatever imperialist institution where he was degrading himself, Kim Il Sung was in the battlefield with a gun at his side and freedom on his mind."

After the outburst, Sun looked around agitated. He knew not the stranger that sat before him though it was the same human being he laughed and joked with during his childhood and for whom he felt an affection for like a brother.

When several moments of silence finally passed, Sun spoke, "So I suppose that you are no longer interested in seeking freedom through the journalistic word?"

Letting out a grunt he replied, "That is nothing more than a bourgeois relic of the past. The only truth I hold is right here," holding his fist to his heart.

Sun continued, "And how long will you be here? It isn't much of anything, but you're welcome to stay at our place if..."

"I told you I came only to have a word with you. In fact, I should be going soon, there is plenty of work that needs to be done."

Sun nodded in understanding, then followed with, "It was good to see you my friend. I worried that you might be dead. You will always be my brother, though you have convinced me of nothing."

"This is my worry. I need you to know, I need you to understand that if anything is to happen, which I can assure you things *will* happen, I cannot protect you. We're encroaching onto something far bigger than ourselves. There will be casualties. Sacrifices must be made. This was my last attempt to try and save you, once the real battle begins..."

"So be it," said Sun standing up after having heard enough, then after a pause, "Take care of yourself."

"You do the same," the freedom fighter replied.

After several awkward moments of silence and having neither embraced nor even bowed to each other, the white-clothed stranger turned around and walked out of the *tabang* just as conspicuously as he had entered it.

As Sun stared at the back of the stranger until he left the *tabang* completely, he said to himself, "Farewell Childong," for now he could finally grieve the death of his childhood friend.

Sa Mi and Sun in Seoul

Sun and his wife left their deteriorating village – held hostage by the constant threat of insurgent uprisings by leftist guerrillas – for a different peril of Seoul. They had decided to pay a visit to the capital upon the advice of their eldest but found only a disheartening sight before them. The streets of Seoul had become flooded with millions of people that had returned from abroad after the end of the occupation, and the capital city could no better welcome the couple than they could those that were aimlessly wandering the streets searching for food. Though key military bases remained, much of the American military had already withdrawn, leaving only a force of GI's to the entertainment of desperate Korean women finding any means necessary to feed their families.

They had brought their youngest child on the journey, so attached she was to her distraught mother. Young slept fitfully for most of the train ride, the fare for which their daughter Mijin had paid. The couple stopped at the orphanage to see their two other children and to bring them as many goodies as they could before their departure. They told them they would only be in Seoul a few days and would come back for them as soon as they returned. The bitterness in their son's eyes had grown sharper and the days apart from their parents had made even the sprightly girl less enthusiastic. Kyu-jin's unruly curls had become limp and flat and she was no longer the feature of curiosity among the children nor did she aspire to be. Sun could barely look at the two children, so sick it made him feel that they had to resort to such measures. His older children had grown up with the excesses of material comforts and it was not as if they loved him or appreciated him any more because of it. He felt equally hated by all of his children, and he felt in many ways as if he deserved every last shred of hostility.

As Hyun watched his parents walk down the familiar dirt road with his baby sister, he abruptly turned his back before they could be seen descending over the hill. When he found his younger sister's tear-streaked face before him, he snapped at her in irritation, "What do you think you're looking at?!"

When the couple and baby descended from the crowded train, they were surprised to find their daughter waiting for them on the platform. Their lovely daughter had the look of dishevelment in her eyes and a vulnerability they had never witnessed before. Marriage, as was often the case in those days, had been cruel to her, and made ever more intolerable by her mother-in-law's insatiable demands. Both Sa Mi and Sun knew that their precious daughter was not used to lifting a finger unless it was to inspect the finery of an object or to purchase one object of affection or other. They had done her no favors in preparing her for marriage by spoiling her so. Sa Mi and Sun had expected to find their eldest son waiting for them as planned. Of course, it was not unusual for Bong-jin to break his engagements, which is why he could never win his father's favor.

"Something came up with *oppa*. He asked me to meet you both here instead," Mijin said with a smile, relieved to see her beloved parents, yet saddened by their defeated state. Accustomed to seeing younger siblings around, Mijin barely acknowledged the sleeping babe in her mother's arms. "How was your trip?" she asked.

186

"As good as can be expected," her father replied, looking around distractedly at the mobs of people and activity that surrounded them.

"It was fine," Sa Mi followed up, "but, how are you? How is our son-in-law?"

"Oh, you know," Mijin replied looking down at the ground, "things have been difficult since father-in-law passed, but we're managing," then noticing her mother's sad eyes she quickly changed the subject, "*oppa* has asked that we go straight to his home..." then after a few beats, "his wife is expecting you know."

At the news of their first grandchild both her parents' eyes lit up for the first time since they had been consumed by their depression, "A grandchild!" Sa Mi exclaimed beaming.

"Perhaps this will make him snap out of his haze and take some responsibility," Sun mumbled to himself.

"I know they would have liked to tell you in person, it's just that, well, sister-in-law hasn't been feeling well and to be honest she wasn't thrilled that you would be coming for a few days so she has been nagging at *oppa* for weeks. Then again, if it isn't one thing that she's upset about it's another, let's just say she may be a little touchy these days. I thought I'd warn you."

At the thought of her precious first-born held mercy by the tongue of *that* woman, Sa Mi glared at her husband who simply looked away.

"And your three younger brothers? How are they?" Sa Mi asked with concern.

"Well, Jong-jin and Yu-jin moved out of *oppa's* house just a few weeks ago," then meeting her mother's even more concerned eyes, "it was getting a little tense in *oppa's* house what with sister-in-law being pregnant now and everything. They decided to move out and share a small room to rent together." Prepared for her mother to ask why they couldn't move in with her, Mijin continued, "You have to understand mother, there was simply no way that I could have made room for them in our house. Mother-in-law has not ceased being after me and," fighting back tears, "we have enough problems of our own and it's been positively exhausting even having Dong-jin stay with us because his stomach is a bottomless pit and it just gives mother-in-law another reason to lash out at me."

Feeling terrible that they had subjected their daughter to such a difficult fate, both parents stayed quiet, not knowing what words to extend to console her. From their perspective, with their pockets dry and their hearts hanging delicately in their wounded chests, they felt they had nothing to offer.

"I'm so sorry my darling," Sa Mi said helplessly, while her father who hated to see his daughter upset echoed the sentiment, "We hope for all this to be a temporary situation. And we thank you for all that you've done."

Mijin quickly wiped away the tears that threatened to fall down her cheek and continued to update her parents on the lives of their children, "It is a much better situation anyway with Jong-jin and Yu-jin on their own. Jong-jin is carrying them both with the money he brings in from tutoring jobs and he is really excelling in school. His English is so good he is looking to find work as a translator on one of the American bases. The two have been fighting like cats and dogs though, Yu-jin has not given up talk about joining a monastery and whenever he mentions it he makes Jong-jin's blood boil. They will join us tonight at *oppa's* house," she added reassuringly, knowing that her parents were anxious to see all of their children.

As they journeyed toward their eldest son's house with their daughter, all the while sharing the words for the times they had spent apart, Sun observed the pulse of life in Seoul which, except for the millions of people, did not seem so different from where he just came from in Damyang. The people had the same pensive look of uncertainty in their eyes and the heat clung to everyone's back like spider webs. The only difference was that the tension was multiplied by the numbers of people. He realized that he and his wife's visit would not turn out to be some saving grace out of the hole they had dug for themselves, but a visit to see how their children were doing, as if to seal in their minds what failures they were as parents. Lost in all of the sights and sounds of Seoul, Sun stepped out of the train having caught only bits and pieces of the conversation between his daughter and his wife. He had his oldest daughter on his mind as the world passed by him, the one that came to him in a bundle of tears one morning many years ago. He wondered how she was and if he'd have the opportunity to see her during their visit to the capital. Sun had written to Soon weeks earlier letting her know that they would be coming for a visit, but he received no reply from the daughter that wished him away.

As they walked among the kicked-up dust of the city, Sun noticed an old man begging passers-by for money or food. Something about the pathetic appearance of the old man caused Sun to gaze intently at his shabby appearance. He wore torn and ragged clothes and leaned on a walking stick. His ragged white beard was gnarled and tangled and the western fishing hat atop his head disguised some of his balding and hid the pain in his eyes. When he looked up, one could see that one eye was inflicted with cataracts while the other searched the world before him. Sun wondered to himself whether he too would end up like that one day. He abruptly interrupted the conversation between his daughter and wife and asked his daughter for a coin, who, upon realizing what her father was doing, clucked her tongue in irritation and dug into her pockets helplessly. Sa Mi glared at her husband who was too preoccupied to notice.

After finding some insignificant coins at the bottom of her pouch, Mijin declared, "Really father! If you stop to give change to every beggar on the street you will leave us in far worse shape than we're already in!"

Ignoring his daughter, Sun approached the old man and placed the two coins in the palm of his hand. Feeling the stranger's contribution, the decrepit man looked up searchingly with his good eye, the other hidden under a haze of cataracts. As his good eye observed Sun curiously, he said in a strong Gwang-ju accent, "It seems we meet again, fellow neighbor!" he declared, then narrowing his good eye further, he lifted his walking stick and started shaking it at Sun, "You bad, bad, bad, bad!" he yelled with his failing vocal chords, the wooden stick flailing in the air.

Sun gasped and backed away, he had recognized him too late and there was no mistaking the old man's voice, it was Meeyoung's father! The maternal grandfather of his first-born daughter! Shaken, Sun quickly retreated back toward his wife and daughter who had witnessed the scene from further away. The old man's cursing seemed to have changed into a weeping holler.

"I *told* you father! You can't just give hand-outs to people like that. This is not Damyang, this is Seoul. Things are different in the big city," she scolded, letting her father know that the times were changing.

Neither mother nor daughter had recognized the old man, but Sun was completely shaken by the incident. After all, there stood who used to be the richest man in Gwangju, who in less than twenty years had become nothing more than a beggar on the street. How long would it take for Sun's dignity to leave him as well? As his daughter took his arm, concerned that her once proud father had aged and suffered much in the years that had ensued, Sun replayed his memories of the old man and his childhood romps with the daughter whose life he was sure he had ruined. As his wife and daughter looked at him with concern, Sun silently walked the rest of the way to his eldest son's home.

As he walked, Sun had one spare moment of clarity that forced him to see the truth of why he could not stand the sight of his son. Like his own father, who had possessed a detached disposition toward him, and who neither favored nor encouraged his tender heart, so did Sun share a disgust for the same tenderness that his son had inherited from him. Life was too cruel to appreciate such a useless characteristic in a man. Such compassion served no purpose but to create illusions when reality was too blinding. Perhaps his friend was right. Sun knew that in his darkest, most honest moments that he was no better than the old man begging on the street. Gambling had distilled an illusion in him that had caused those he loved much pain and heartache. And yet, he was a slave to that illusion, unable to let go of it if nothing to ease the suffering of his family, much less to free himself. He had the sinking feeling that the illusions his eldest son harbored would destroy him as well. Sun hoped with all his heart that he was wrong.

When they finally reached Bong-jin's home, the couple found only their irritable daughter-in-law fighting to hide the fact that she was not thrilled to greet her in-laws. In those days, it was typically Sa Mi's role as mother-in-law, aided by her own daughter, to be sure that the life of her son's wife was made more miserable from marriage. (This was the unbearable situation in which her own daughter found herself.) Given the current circumstances however, Sa Mi felt ashamed by her daughter-in-law's cold greeting and did not feel emboldened to punish her for her disrespect. After all, it was no secret that her son could not hold a steady job and that it was his wife's parents that kept the couple afloat. Sa Mi knew that their own desperate situation which led her and her husband to Seoul that day had not gone unnoticed by the girl's parents, for surely her daughter-in-law had complained about this very fact to them. Even if Sa Mi had possessed the cranky, demanding disposition of most mothers-in-law, or if she had suffered the same cruelty herself and harbored the bitterness of such a plight, she would have nothing to say to this homely, unpleasant girl before her, though Sa Mi continued to curse Sun for arranging her precious son's marriage to her in the first place. Sa Mi turned to give him an eye, but he was too distracted by his own thoughts to notice.

Mijin, on the other hand, who suffered much under the sour and vindictive tongue of her own mother-in-law and rarely caught a glimpse of the sweet light of freedom, seized the power that society gave her in her brother's house to release some of her own frustration.

"And where is my brother?" she asked accusingly to her sister-in-law who, like her own mother, Mijin detested from the very beginning. "I hope you have not driven him out yet again, especially on the day his own parents and your *shi-omonee* and *shi-aboji* have arrived from their long journey."

Unable to hide the loathing that she had for her husband's sister, the cantankerous ball of a woman replied, "But *agasshi*, surely even you are aware of your brother's needs to quench his thirst outside the home. I do not allow a drop of alcohol in the house and your sweet brother just couldn't seem to wait a moment longer. I'm sure he'll be back soon," she curled her voice looking straight at Mijin. She was not going to go down from her sister-in-law's antics.

"Well, I'm sure he went to get father some rice wine, *everybody* knows father loves rice wine and wouldn't it have been nice to have some ready for him after his long journey?" Then clicking her tongue, "Alcohol or no alcohol, I have a very good idea of what *my* father-in-law enjoys and I know I have it ready for him every time he walks in through the door."

Sun raised the palm of his hand to put a stop to the raucous and insisted that he was just fine. By this time his daughter-in-law had laid cups of tea and fresh cut apples under their noses. Taking a sip of the tea Sun followed up with, "This is exactly what I needed, just perfect. I don't want any wine, it will only add to my tiredness."

An awkward silence followed as everyone glanced at one another uncomfortably. Seeing that her child was now awake, Sa Mi propped her up to a sitting position as the girl gazed at everyone intently. Sun, who had never expressed much affection toward his children, lest it was through intimidation or the pity he saved for his oldest daughter, lifted the girl up in the air and planted a kiss on her round cheeks. In his bruised state, Sun had managed to find solace in this youngest child of his. Her gaze touched him somewhere deep inside. Everyone paused to watch this unusual display from the man who preferred the company of adults to the chaos of children. Mijin, in particular, took notes as it struck her that though she captured her father's fondness early on, she was no match for the adorable babe in her father's arms for whom his softened brow and years of life had revealed a loving tenderness that she had never before witnessed. She couldn't help feeling a tinge of jealousy toward her baby sister. After all, given her own suffering in the prison of her marriage, Mijin craved her parents' attention more than anything.

Sa Mi decided she would break the silence, "So, we hear that we should be expecting our first grandchild soon?" she inquired of her daughter-in-law with a smile.

"Oh, oh yes," her daughter-in-law replied glancing at Mijin who was surely the one who had spilled the beans, "yes, I am with child," she added with very little emotion.

"What a wonderful gift!" Sa Mi said, over-exaggerating her enthusiasm to make up for the lack of enthusiasm in her daughter-in-law's voice.

"Yes, we are very happy," Sun added distractedly, bouncing the baby girl on his leg.

Right then they heard voices at the front gate and Sa Mi stood up, prepared to greet her precious oldest son. Her husband remained sitting with the babe while Mijin stood up quickly as well. The miserable daughter-in-law stood up only reluctantly.

The front door burst open as Sa Mi's oldest son fired through the door with open arms, in his hand was a half full bottle of rice wine which his sister intercepted as he greeted his mother and father.

"*Omonee, aboji*," Bong-jin cried out and bowed as his mother embraced him lovingly. He then approached his father and bowed respectfully as Sun glanced his eyes up and only mumbled, "I see you're here," as he continued to play with his *mangnae*. Everyone could smell the faintness of *soju* on the eldest's breath, something they had grown accustomed to over the years.

Sa Mi was elated to see that her oldest son was trailed by her three other sons, the two who lived and quarreled with each other, and the chubby fourth son who stayed with her daughter. All bowed respectfully to their parents, showcasing their characteristic demeanors. Though he only coldly acknowledged his oldest, Sun saw fit to stand up for the rest (more out of curiosity than of affection) and he handed his babe to Mijin for the time being.

His second son, Jong-jin, was the first to approach. Sun was partial to Jong-jin who had adopted his likeness without all of his vices and who was gifted with a sharp and studious brain. Jong-jin's facial expressions reflected this sharpness and his angular features were further exaggerated by his square glasses. In many ways, this son resembled the son he had left behind in Damyang under the care of the orphanage. The thought of his two children there humbled him as Jong-jin bowed respectfully to his father though not without an air of arrogance. Sun let the offense pass unnoticed, he knew from his wife that the boy was working hard to support himself and his brother while excelling in his own studies. Fatherly guilt prevented him from saying anything to this industrious son.

Next was his son Yu-jin who Sun knew very little about. He was, for the most part, indifferent toward this son who reminded him of some kind of wallowing artist without the requisite credentials. The boy had shaved his head and Sun knew he had been talking about joining a monastery so when Yu-jin approached him with a bow, Sun took it upon himself to give the boy a light smack on the head followed by a, "What is this?"

"Father, I am preparing myself to join the way of the Buddha," he replied simply.

He had barely gotten the words out when Sun interjected with disdain, "Only the weak need religion. You better wake up and help out your brother more with the living expenses," he said with disgust, then shooed him away as if the mere sight of him caused him suffering.

When Sa Mi's chubby, fourth son approached her with a bow, it nearly broke her heart in two. He was the slowest of all her children and Sa Mi would blame herself for it until she reached the grave, for it was when she was pregnant with Dong-jin when the chaos of children and the loneliness of her existence had compelled her to take abortive herbs and to fall down on purpose, in order to put a stop to the cycle of motherhood that plagued her since marriage. It was the first time since she ran and ran as a young girl that she tried to fight against Fate and it would be the last, for the baby was born despite her efforts and three more would be born after him.

When the chubby boy bowed to his father, Sun looked at him as if he was a stranger. Dong-jin did not resemble him at all, nor did he necessarily resemble his wife, so as he stood there, Sun simply looked down at him without words.

"Good to see you," he said finally, feeling a touch of pity toward Dong-jin whom he never knew and who was clearly the slowest in mental and physical attributes out of all his children.

After all the greetings had been exchanged, everyone took a seat once again and the expression on Bong-jin's wife's face had turned from annoyance to contempt at the sight of her jovial husband. Bong-jin handed his father a glass first and was about to pour him some of his favorite rice wine when Sun said, "I don't want any," waving his hand away.

"But father…" the young man replied in vain, knowing that he would never be the son his father had hoped for.

"I don't want any," Sun replied again, his anger mounting and his eyes narrowing at his eldest.

This created another uncomfortable pause and as everyone else attempted idle conversation with one another, Sun sat with a wedge between himself and tender-hearted Bong-jin.

"Father, I am sorry…" the eldest started, trying to apologize for being late and not greeting his parents at the train station as promised.

"What kind of eldest son doesn't even greet his parents when they are coming from a long journey?!" Sun asked accusingly, "What good is an eldest son anyway? You are nothing to me!" he continued, his anger unraveling.

Knowing Sun's temper, especially when it came to his oldest son, everyone in the room felt that it would be a long, first night together. Bong-jin stood awkwardly with a bottle of wine in his hand and an insatiable thirst for alcohol that seemed to be the only remedy to his father's deep contempt for him and his wife's constant nagging. Perhaps his father was right, perhaps he only knew him too well. He would be nothing more in this life but a tender heart walking around with a desperate thirst for the bottle.

And really, there was nothing more useless in a man than the combination of those two things. Nobody knew this better than Bong-jin himself.

Waiting

D espite what his pride dictated, Hyun looked out the
orphanage window every morning to see if his parents
might be walking down that dusty dirt road for him and his
sister. Each day that he did not see them the bitterness in his heart
extended another prick in his soul that reverberated all the way to
his icy toes. He isolated himself in the solace of his books while his
sister played with the other children and occasionally made futile
attempts to communicate with him. The sight of her now matted,
flat head of hair which used to be full of curls only added to his
misery and her attempts to fraternize with him were always met
with the bitterness that he held close to his heart. With every day
that passed, the hostility Hyun nursed was transforming into a
way of being that became more and more resistant to change. The
object of his disdain could be placed squarely on the image of his
parents walking away. Like for everything in his life that was
made to be raw and painful, Hyun blamed his parents. How could
they be so foolish to think that a hunger in their bellies could
distract them from a hunger in their heart?

They seemed to him to be a ridiculous pair, an anachronistic
one who knew little about the bare bones of survival. And even as
a young boy he had developed a healthy disrespect for those who
couldn't rely on their God-given logic to solve problems. Along
with many others Hyun placed his parents in this category. In his

eyes they simply were not up to the challenge of survival, to change, to adapting to what the world placed in front of them. Early on he had decided that he could respect someone no matter their disposition so long as they worked hard and could competently manage their affairs. Everybody else he hadn't the time for.

One morning as he conducted his ritual gaze out the window, he spotted the couple coming down the dirt road toward the orphanage with his baby sister. The pair looked even more pitiable than when he had last seen them. They had told him before they last left them that they were going to Seoul to visit his brothers and sister and to see if there were any opportunities for them there. By the looks of them it was apparent that no such opportunities existed. Hyun took this as a sign that he and his sister would be stuck in that jail cell indefinitely. As they approached, Hyun turned his back toward the window in scorn.

Minutes later his younger sister came to him squealing in delight, "Mother and father are here! They've come for us!" she declared.

"They're probably only here for a visit, I wouldn't hold your breath," he advised. Hyun then sat down on the floor and opened a book as to appear at the peak of disinterest when they arrived. As his younger sister ran out the front door to greet them, Hyun stayed put. He stared down at his book as they walked toward him.

"*Aii-yah*, poor thing," he heard his mother lament when she caught a glimpse of him, "He has his head buried in a book," she pointed out to her husband.

Sun's father responded with praise that he reserved only for this son, "Yes, yes he is a good boy. He will be someone very special in the future."

Hyun continued to act as if he was too absorbed in his reading material to notice the couple.

Finally, Sa Mi spoke up, "*Hyun-a*, your mother and father are here for you."

"We're going home!" squealed his sister excitedly clinging onto Sa Mi's skirt.

Hyun looked up at his parents for the first time with a measured look of indifference. "Are we really going home?" he asked as if their interruption had caused him an inconvenience in his studying.

"Yes," Sa Mi responded, "Come. Let's get your things together. Your brother Jong-jin has been working so hard, his generosity should keep us afloat for at least a little while. He gave us a little something especially for you and your sisters, so come on," Sa Mi exclaimed hurriedly.

Hyun knew better than to think that his second oldest had said anything about his younger siblings knowing how detached he was in general. His detachment however, did not get in the way of his sense of duty, and he more often than not compensated for what Hyun's oldest brother lacked. Hyun knew that Jong-jin's gesture of giving his parents money was just another example of Jong-jin filling in out of a sense of responsibility. Nonetheless, while he didn't show it, Hyun was grateful for it. He put his eldest brother in the same category that he put his parents: unable to cope and therefore unworthy of respect.

Hyun methodically packed his bag with his books and his meticulously folded clothes, not allowing his mother to touch his items, but doing everything himself.

His father praised him again, so impressed he was by his son's neatness and independent attitude, "So organized," he exclaimed, "very good, yes, he will definitely do something special with his life."

Such comments from his father only irritated him more as they still lived in a society where a child's hope rested on the opportunities that his parents afforded him. What had his parents offered him except abandonment when times grew difficult? Hyun decided that if he was ever going to do anything with his life it would require a great deal of luck and the iron will he had already begun cultivating. If anything good were to happen with his life, it would have to be his own doing and would have nothing to do with his parents.

Meanwhile, as he watched his son pack his items, Sun pondered what they could do with the money that Jong-jin had given them. It pained Sun to see the bright, gifted boy before him alongside his own sad state of affairs, not to mention his inability to keep up with the children's school fees. The children never mentioned anything to him, but Sun imagined they suffered humiliation when they were called by the teachers to pay their dues.

How could he have ever let anything get to this point? Sun felt at that moment that his losing streak was over and if he could just play his hands right he could turn that small change into something big, and that his kids could go to school again with dignity. He fought this temptation with all of his might and even gave the money to his wife to hold on to, so frightening was the urge to go to the gambling hall and do what he knew best. But no matter how much he tried to quell that beast inside of him it continued to resurface and bubble over into his mind. There was always that possibility that he could turn the money into something, to make it grow, whereas if they used it in their daily lives, it would run out eventually, and soon at that. He recalled his wife's words as she placed the money into her pouch, "We *need* this money," she pleaded with her eyes, "We don't know what's going to happen," she had said with a worried tone.

He knew exactly what she was referring to. The trip to Seoul had proved disheartening to their sense of where the country was headed. By now the Americans had left and there was a general malaise among the population. Sun realized that Gwangju province wasn't the only politically unstable hotbed in the country, but that underneath the whole peninsula was a rippling tide, threatening to implode. Nobody wanted a country severed in two, and there were too many different opinions about what a unified Korea should be. Sun and Sa Mi had hurried home from Seoul to go back to what was familiar. Something about the mounting pressure in the city haunted them, and Sa Mi wanted to retrieve her younger children from the orphanage as soon as possible. There they stood: not knowing how to contend with the density of the air and the uncertainty of what was to come. Sun eyed his talented son with a vulnerability he had never before revealed.

After thanking the staff and bidding them farewell, the couple then left the orphanage with their three youngest children by their side. By this time the *mangnae*, Young, possessed a pink glow to her round cheeks, had put on weight to the satisfaction of her parents, and though she could walk, her mother still held onto her contented body. A spring in her spirit livened up the curls of their other daughter who clung onto her mother's skirt and talked incessantly about her adventures at the orphanage. Hyun remained quiet. He took one last look over his shoulder at the building at the bottom of the hill. He had the nagging feeling that it would not be the last time that he would lay eyes on it.

The Invasion

June 1950

In Seoul, Hyun's older siblings were in disarray. Once the rumors were confirmed that the North Korean army had indeed crossed the 38th parallel and were en route to Seoul, Sun's oldest son Bong-jin and his pregnant wife had decided to join the trail of refugees heading south, back to their home town in Damyang. Though it was a long journey and all modes of major transportation had been stopped, the irritable wife's parents who had important connections, arranged for the couple to be driven at least some of the way by a US military vehicle. Unlike her husband who had become quite adapted to city life, the petulant young woman never got used to it nor did she get used to all of her husband's pestering siblings. She was more than ready to be home and in the company of her own parents. So when her husband suggested that they invite his siblings along for the journey, she furiously objected.

"Absolutely not! I am so tired of your family trying to coast along the kindness and generosity of my parents! Can't they think for themselves and find their own way out of this mess?" she lashed out.

"I don't feel right about leaving my brothers with my sister's family. They are my responsibility."

"*You*? You're talking about responsibility? How funny! And what about the responsibility to your wife?! And when was the last time you've tried to do anything to better our situation without it blowing up in our faces? It's always *my* parents that bail us out of the mess that *you* created. And *your* parents? They come up here like beggars trying to get money from us!"

"That's not true," the chiseled face responded, his features getting sharper as his wife's words took biting stabs at his pride. "They came up here to see their children and to see if there were any opportunities for them here, I told them to come up."

"Yes, *you* told them. And what a brilliant idea that turned out to be! They came here for money, they came here like beggars!"

Unable to bear his wife's screeches any longer, Bong-jin bolted out of the house as her screams followed him out the door. He walked through the city all the way near where the university was and knocked on the door of the building where his younger brothers were sharing a room.

Fortunately, they were both there. The younger one with the shaved head and a yearning for enlightenment answered the door.

"*Hyeong!*" he declared, happy to see his older brother whom he hadn't seen since their parents had left.

The other brother who sat at the desk, glanced up and nodded his head, but continued reading.

Bong-jin entered their room and instructed Jong-jin to put the book away. "Listen," he started, "My in-laws have arranged a military vehicle to take us out of Seoul and back to Damyang until everything settles down around here. I want you two and Dong-jin to come with us."

The shaved head looked up at his older brother with interest, Yu-jin had become disillusioned with life in the city. Jong-jin however, had eyes that did not shift behind his black spectacles and simply said, "And then what?"

"What do you mean, 'and then what'? We don't know what's going to happen here, and you should be with your family."

"I'm not going," Jong-jin replied flatly.

The shaved head felt compelled to interject, "Perhaps *hyeong* is right. Maybe we should leave with them and come back later, you know, until things get straightened out."

The studious brother who wore the confidence of his scholarship repeated again, "You can do whatever you want, but I am not going. I'm going to stay here and wait to see what happens. There's nothing for me in Damyang."

The other two brothers looked at each other. They knew that once Jong-jin's mind was made up there was no changing it, and besides, with his intelligence and talent he was the only one out of all of them that could be able to make something of himself. He was right. Their small village had nothing to offer him.

"I guess I'm staying behind with *hyeong* then," Yu-jin responded, for though he clashed often with his brother, his loyalty to him always won in the end.

Just then they heard a frantic knock at the door and the voice of their sister Mijin. "*Bong-jin ya!*" she called out, knowing that her older brother was there in the room.

When they opened the door to let her in they found their normally graceful sister in a shattered state, followed by their chubby younger brother who was not one for many words.

Mijin looked like she had been crying. Her brothers asked her what was wrong. Embarrassed to have her younger brothers see her in such a state, she reached for her older brother and pulled him outside of the cramped quarters.

"Your wife said I could probably find you here," she managed to say in her weakened voice, "she told me that you were all going back to Damyang."

"Yes, yes that's right, I came here to see if our brothers would go, but they refused. But I'll take Dong-jin with us so he is off your hands..."

"Take me too!" she called out desperately, pleading with her older brother behind teary eyes.

Never one to say "no" to any of his loved ones, the young man thought to himself about whether there would be enough room with his sister's family and he and his wife. "Of course, we will find a way to make this work, don't worry about it," he said to comfort his pained sister. "Is your mother-in-law going to be okay for the journey?" he inquired, knowing that her health had been failing as of late.

"No!" Mijin cried out, "No, no, no, no, not *her*," she emphasized, "not *him* either," she said referring to her husband, "just me and Dong-jin. I never want to see either of them again!" she declared with conviction.

Shocked to see how upset his sister was and how sure she was about her decision, Bong-jin made one last attempt, "Look, you're just upset right now, I'm sure whatever it is it will blow over, just..."

"No!" she responded firmly, "Never. Please, just let me go with you, if it is not with you I will walk all the way to my parents' home, I don't care if my feet bleed and fall off. I am not staying in that house any longer," she added.

Seeing as how she didn't volunteer what had happened that had prompted her to such a state of desperation, Bong-jin did not press any further, but nodded his head in acquiescence.

"Of course you can come with us," he replied, "just come with Dong-jin and meet us back home in a couple hours. Don't bring too much stuff," he warned.

The relief in his sister's eyes comforted him and she thanked him as she grabbed their younger brother and hurried home to prepare for the journey south.

Bong-jin went back inside his brothers' room and made one last plea to Jong-jin and Yu-jin. He then told them about their sister and that he wasn't sure when they would be back. There was a comfort to such obvious statements, though no one dared to make explicit all the Communist horror stories in their minds, including that young boys like Jong-jin and Yu-jin would get conscripted by the North Korean army. They kept silent about such possibilities and exchanged quick goodbyes before Bong-jin hurried home to make preparations for the journey and to find a way to tell his wife that his younger sister and brother were accompanying them. He stood for an awkward moment in front of his brothers. Bong-jin's pockets were empty except for some coins he was saving for a much-needed drink before he went home. He had nothing to offer them. The two boys understood as they had been in that very same awkward situation many times before so they eased the exchange by hurrying him out and telling him that they would write.

"You'd better get home before your wife gives you an earful," said the bespectacled brother who patted his *hyeong* on the shoulder in a rare show of affection. And with that Bong-jin was out the door for a couple of hits of *soju* before he went home to deal with his wife and the preparations.

It wouldn't be until much later that Bong-jin and the rest of his family would learn the truth behind his sister's tears. While it was bad enough that she had been suffering under the wrath of her mother-in-law and her husband's indifference, nothing would prepare her for the scandal that broke out when it was revealed that the charming English teacher who at one time had inspired all the silly love songs over the gramophone to play over and over in her head, had been bestowing his charms onto a sixteen-year-old student who also swooned at the sound of his voice. To make matters worse, the young girl was with his child. But that is another story. And for the moment, there is a war overshadowing all of these lives.

The Wolves

The time had come. Soon sat in front of her vanity running her hairbrush through her silken locks. Her gaze remained unchanged throughout the years. Soon wore the same stony disposition of her youth, and despite the hardship of the years, the stubborn beauty she inherited from her mother and grandmother remained intact.

She had been sheltered from the upheaval leading up to this moment. Her father had served her well by marrying her to a good man, a reliable man, a man who cared for her and shielded her from the dramas of the outside world. He bought her a home perched high on a hill and gave her everything he could afford and that she desired. With his remaining time, the decorated and dependable military officer sought to build up the South Korean army. It was a nearly impossible feat, especially after the Americans left the peninsula despite Syngman Rhee's repeated pleas that the U.S. forces stay and help unify the peninsula under one government. General Shin was a patriot in every sense, and his blind and earnest devotion to his beautiful wife and country was evident to all who knew him.

Over the years, Soon became her husband's biggest supporter and sounding board. At first, the General was tickled by his wife's interest in his affairs, but soon, her keen observations and attentive ear drew him closer to her. He shared everything with her, and she reflected back thoughtful insights, encouragement, and wise and informed counsel. He became all the more enamored to his lovely wife as a result of these exchanges. The General found that his wife seemed to have more military prowess and strategic thinking than his most trusted advisors. So, to the ignorance of the highly-placed political and military strategists that served the General and the President, Yi Soonjin, the illegitimate daughter of the proud Yi Sun Soo, was dictating the military strategies and policies of the inchoate South Korean government.

Having been thoroughly seduced by his beautiful wife, the General sought to strengthen and build up the fledgling army with renewed inspiration and an appreciation for the dumb luck to have married someone with both beauty and intelligence. Soon was a young woman who never nagged, never complained, and was always there for him after his long hours at work. Her apparent dedication to her husband never made him think twice of the vast amount of time that was left to Soon during his prolonged work days, and the General never pondered how she could possibly be using that time. They didn't have children, and neither one of them showed an interest or concern in their lack of a child, despite the General's family's disapproval of their childless state. That Soon was taking herbs to prevent such a pregnancy to occur was just another secret she kept from her husband. She had decided long ago that she would never bring a child into the world, for she saw only suffering in her own childhood experiences, and she now had her sights on a far greater goal. How could the General have been so naïve to think that a woman who shared such sharp and incisive insights into the details of political maneuvering and strategizing, would be sitting at home every day waiting for his return?

In fact, Yi Soonjin had a very busy schedule, and her days were full and industrious. She saw to her commitments just as soon as her husband left the house. This day was not much different than the rest. Soon smartly placed barrettes in her hair and a pillbox hat atop her head. She reviewed the notes that she had written down in code earlier in the morning, then placed them at the bottom of a basket under two handkerchiefs, atop of which she placed some shiny red apples. The notes elucidated recent conversations with her husband regarding the army's status and preparations against a northern attack. There were details regarding the South Korean army's intelligence regarding whether they perceived a threat, and what they would do if one were to occur. The main points were that the fledging army was ill-prepared, had contradicting intelligence, and that there was dissension among the ranks. All this was meticulously captured in Comrade Yi Soonjin's scrupulous handwriting and hidden behind an indecipherable code, conspicuously bearing the weight of apples.

As always, Soon put on her white gloves, picked up her basket and walked out of her bedroom looking immaculate. She said nothing to the maid as she left the house, who was the only person that was suspicious of her master's whereabouts every day. Soon then made her way to the American base in Seoul that had all but been abandoned to a small group of U.S. forces who were eager to follow their fellow servicemen back home.

Even stony Soon could barely hide her anticipation as she walked the streets of Seoul, a hop in her step, and the clunk of her heels breaking the taut tension throughout the city. Among the servicemen that had been left behind was Sergeant First Class John Murphy from Waterloo, Iowa. Handsome, strapping, young and lonely, the brave Sergeant Murphy had crossed paths with Soon at a social gathering for her husband. They had locked eyes from across the room and when Soon introduced herself to him before she left, she slipped him a piece of paper with instructions to meet her at a teahouse the following day. Ever reliable, and never one to turn down the invitation of a beautiful woman, of which he received many, the two began meeting at seedy hotels near the base. It was on Soon's insistence. Even good wholesome John had tried to talk her out of it.

"I have some money, let's get a room over at the Chosun Hotel, where the diplomats stay. You're far too classy for this place. I don't want to bring you here anymore."

Soon, who understood every English word, having studied it along with Mandarin for the past few years, (another secret she kept from her husband), simply placed her index finger over his lips, locked eyes with him, and used her other hand to unbutton his battle fatigues, so she could stroke her delicate hand along his chest.

To say he was utterly beguiled by her was an understatement. He had never met anyone like her in his twenty years. She was equally intrigued by him, which for Soon, who never deigned to give anyone the slightest consideration, was truly something. Their attraction to each other was mutual and magnetic from the very start. That she had intended to use him to gather more intelligence almost became an afterthought. He was a lousy informant besides, he never gave up anything, not because he possessed any shred of skepticism, or suspected Soon in the least, it was that he was so *good*, so very honest and sincere. It's almost as if he felt it bad manners to talk shop with her. John was interested only in Soon. Their time together was a haven against the backdrop of upheaval and smoke. He didn't want to discuss politics, or all the muddied legacies of power, colonialism, and ideology that brought him there in the first place. John was the only American that Soon had ever come across, and she wondered to herself whether all Americans were as ingenuous as her GI. And if so, she pondered, it ought to be rather quick and painless to unify the peninsula under a Communist regime.

When she tried to steer the conversation to American policy, the only thing he ever said was, "They say we're going home soon, Soon," with a twinkle in his eye, but his voice was tinged with regret. For John Murphy opposed the no-win outcome of the Korean peninsula after World War II, severed at the 38th parallel, and having to compromise with the Soviets. Ever the brave American soldier, he wanted to finish the job. Take the peninsula. Drive out all the commies. Only then would John feel assured saying "farewell" to his lover. Only then could he feel good about returning her country back to her.

Soon looked around before knocking on the door. She had barely rapped once before John swung the door open and swooped her into his arms. He took the basket of apples from her and placed it on the nightstand. Then he gently laid Soon out on the bed and proceeded to make love to her with a passion he had only discovered with her. It was a passion that ran latent in him all his life among the rows of cornfields and endless Midwestern skies. A passion that remained buried among the staid, hard-working, Protestant sensibility of his birthplace. When he won all-state two years in a row as his high school's star quarterback and everyone congratulated him, he responded with, "Well, thank you very much Mr. and Mrs...." and, "That's very kind of you..." He was all manners all the time, so when he made love to his girlfriend Jenny back home, he checked in with her continuously, more concerned with her satisfaction than his own. But with Soon he was entirely different, together their bodies melded into one. John wanted so much to know Soon, to save Soon and the shadows beyond her gaze, but he knew this was as close as he could get to her. So, he made the most of it.

After they had whittled away most of the morning in this manner, Soon got dressed again and did not linger as she usually did. John watched her with interest.

"What are you doing with that basket of apples? You're like little red riding hood... Do you know the story of little red riding hood?" he asked with the signature twinkle in his eye.

Soon half smiled and lifted her eyes from her nylons, sometimes this was enough to acknowledge John without having to put all the English words together. She knew he enjoyed it when she practiced her English on him though and added, "They are for a special friend, nice fresh apples," she responded with mystery, then, "And no, I do not know your little red riding hood."

"It's a fairy tale," he replied, not having abandoned his curiosity for the recipient of her shiny apples, "an old child's story, about a little girl bringing food for her sick grandmother, only to find that a wolf had gotten to her first. The wolf had dressed up as the grandmother so it could eat little red riding hood too when she approached."

Then reaching over to push a tendril of hair from the side of her face, John added tenderly in her ear, "You're my little red riding hood. I have to protect you."

His tone struck the faintest chord in Soon, subtle, but noticeable. She placed her hand on top of his and smiled, "Protect me? From who? The wolf? Maybe protect me from myself?" she added slyly before turning around to slip on her jacket.

John let out a measured sigh. "Leaving so soon?" Then, understanding that this was the nature of their unions, too brief, desirous, and discreet, "Just watch out for wolves out there," he said, understanding there were things about his lover that were simply unknowable. Then standing up, he added, "I mean it, be careful Soon, things are...stirring. Don't linger around the streets."

There was that faint chord again, tugging on her heart. Soon realized that she'd better get out of there. She kissed him on his lips, then looked him in eyes for the last time, "Watch out for the wolves too," she said, then turned around and closed the door.

That Soon stopped by to see John before delivering her basket of apples revealed that she was not all calculation and coldness. One might even say her behavior was reckless, certainly not conduct that the Party would have condoned. It was clear that John was not a good source of information, yet she sought him again and again like a drug, as if she needed to test her own commitment to the Party. She had certainly provided them with a wealth of information over the past few years. The final tidbit of information which lay underneath the apples, added to what the North already knew to be true and solidified their conviction to roll across the border five days later. And when the Communists captured Seoul three days after that, Soon was ready for them, greeting them with a wave of the red flag.

Sergeant First Class John Murphy was never sent home to the wide expanse of the Midwestern plains, but stayed through the ensuing months to help recapture Seoul in September 1950. He never felt further away from Iowa then during those bloody times. The battles took place in the city, and along the same streets that Soon would plod down from her house on the hill to meet him. The Marines engaged in house-to-house combat with a heavily-armed Northern army. Dust, dirt, blood, screams.

John recalled the dead quiet of the Midwestern evenings at dusk, the gentle roll of the tips of the prairie grass, and the neat, orderly rows of corn that faded into the horizon. Here there was only shrapnel and treachery. He fought back memories of his times with Soon, and the anodyne she was to his loneliness, and the balm they were to each other. John couldn't comprehend anything more than that. He simply couldn't wrap his mind around it, that he was nothing more to her than a means of information. He chose to believe that she was his little red riding hood, and that he simply couldn't save her in the end. Soon's image continued to haunt him long after he finally returned home to the cornfields and endless horizons as a decorated war hero and people would ask, "Where's Korea again?" then proceed to go about their business, tending to the orderly rows of corn, and the security of small town American life. Meanwhile, there was a space in Sergeant First Class Murphy that could never be reached.

Once it was revealed that he had been betrayed by his own wife, Soon's husband, General Shin, the shining patriot, was gunned down as a traitor by his men. These were chaotic times, violent and harrowing, for no one knew who the wolves were, and preemptive killing served as insurance. Soon was able to escape such a fate and joined her fellow comrades during the invasion, never to set foot in that house on the hill again.

Young-jin: Beloved *Mangnae*

We still do not fully understand the effect of violence on young children. For children in war-torn countries who have only ever known the screech of shrapnel, the dearth of basic necessities, the constant fear and tension of the adults around them, the endless anticipation, and the imminent escape, each day brings further dread, something else to fear. In the West Bank, Aleppo, Mosul, Mogadishu, we are raising a generation that has only known the vacuum of war and uncertainty.

Young-jin, the solemn babe who was Sa Mi's youngest and beloved *mangnae*, who languished as a baby the first time her mother dropped her off at the orphanage in the care of others while her older brother turned his back in anguish, would attest later that she had no memory of the time period of the Korean War. She was too young she would say, and that the fortunate coincidence of the timing of her birth spared her the trauma of war. Young-jin, as she herself surmised decades later, had no memory of the war and was therefore not a victim of it; unlike her husband, ten years her senior, who remembered too much and too vividly.

Among the memories that eluded Young-jin was this one: In the summer of 1950 rumors began to spread, and blood began to shed, as refugees came pouring south. Despite repeated announcements over the radio that the South Korean government was holding the line and that Seoul would not be given up, the North Koreans had not only captured the capital city but were well on their way down South. President Syngman Rhee and his government had already fled the capital, leaving a recorded message on the airwaves of false hope, abandoning his citizens to cope in the ensuing chaos.

Sa Mi and Sun were frantic. Sa Mi had lost all communications with her older children in Seoul and knew not about their whereabouts. Their region had always been a hotbed of subversive activity, and as communist guerillas emerged from their homes to join the fray, it was evident that Sa Mi and Sun would need to go into hiding immediately. That their lives were in danger under a communist assault given their political leanings and ties was a foregone conclusion.

But what to do with their three youngest children? The youngest, Young-jin, had grown from a solemn babe to an iron-willed five-year old, wearing the same proud demeanor of her eldest half-sister, though with the stalwart affirmation that she was the legitimate progeny of her family's storied legacy; and unlike her eldest half-sister, who loathed her father and stepmother with a vivid torment and framed her life to inflict daggers onto them and their shared name, Young-jin was her parents' fiercest defender.

Unlike her older siblings, Young-jin never knew the benefits of her family name and the abundance and comfort that her family once enjoyed. Her existence had only been colored by hardship, want, and chaos. The past didn't mean much to Young-jin and that it hung onto her parents so stubbornly irritated her. She observed the world with a skeptical eye and a conservative heart, always exercising restraint as she watched her mother's interactions with others, so open, so honest, so ingenuous, during a time of deceit and betrayal.

Having grown up in such a background, and with a character to never be able to hold her tongue, Young-jin would openly challenge her parents, question their behavior, and point out contradictions. Sun, who was not used to having his children disrespect him in any way, never having tolerated such assaults, had nothing to say to his youngest child who was wise beyond her five years and who boldly held a mirror in front of him, showing him all his insecurities and flaws in plain view. He simply nodded and grunted a bit, succumbing to the moral certainty of her gaze.

Young-jin's frankness was paralleled by her loyalty to the two pillars before her. Ever since birth, she never left their side. While her brother Hyun-jin was buried in a book to psychically escape the hurt from his parents and the times, or her sister Kyu-jin was seeking the company of other children, Young was on guard of her parents, interjecting as necessary, but seeking to deter the stress and anxiety that pervaded them. That their lives were in peril became more and more palpable as the Northern army marched south, and Young, sensing the danger, sought to alleviate the impending doom by never leaving their side, never letting them out of her sight, by abandoning her five-year-old sensibilities, and being a mature big girl, by being grown, by being a leader in her family when the dangers of the world were descending onto her parents, the very ones who were supposed to protect her. She would need to protect them.

Recall that Young professes to have no memory of any of these times. That as an adult she would state that the Korean War and the events leading up to it had occurred when "she was a baby," and that she was spared the loss and pain experienced by her older siblings. Was she telling the truth? Did she truly have no memories of being a five, six, seven-year-old? Is this what we can expect from children in war zones? That trauma simply leaves a black stain of memory? Or is trauma the pain that her brother Hyun-jin nursed all his life?

In any case, at this point, there was no time for deliberation. Out in the streets, fire and smoke had begun to erupt, and Sa Mi and Sun ran through the streets of Gwangju, their three youngest children in tow, sprinting toward the orphanage at the bottom of the hill with their heads down. The edifice was in disarray and the orphanage staff sought to manage the crisis and to accommodate all the children being brought to them. Some missionaries had arrived from Europe and America and had assembled a cross at the front of the building as if it would shelter them from the disaster outside.

Young, having only been a baby the last time she was at the orphanage looked around in confusion. Hyun and Kyu-jin, who were all too familiar with the orphanage, and the feelings of abandonment and the despair that accompanied it, were speechless and somewhat resigned to their fate.

When the possibility closed in around five-year-old Young that the two people for whom she was responsible could leave without her – the two for whom she stood guard, the curious man and woman who seemed so out of place in these times, the only times with which she was familiar, times of treachery and betrayal which required a skeptic's approach, times during which she would need to guide her parents, help them, protect them – her heart dropped. When she finally realized they were leaving her behind, making themselves vulnerable to the uncertainties of the world, Young screamed and grabbed hold of them. A white woman with a cross around her neck pulled her away, murmuring in a foreign language as Young continued to fight, kicking her legs, as she reached out to her parents. She needed to protect them. It was her one certainty.

"*Omma!*" she cried, "*Appa!*" she screamed to no avail. She felt her older brother's hand on her, and saw a tear roll down under his eyeglasses. He was trembling. It would be the only time she would ever witness such vulnerability from him. Young couldn't see the faces of her parents, they dared not turn around. Out the door they went, with Young screaming in their wake.

Young remembers none of this however. And only a black stain remains in place of memory.

Unlike her brother, who had long turned his back from the window and the image of their parents walking away, Young stayed glued to the theater framed by the window for any indication of her parents. Whether her eyes registered the violent skirmishes before her is unclear, including an incident where a group of guerrillas had captured three policemen and taken them out into the street. The captors made the men kneel down before slicing both sides of their faces then shooting them in the back of their heads.

The staff tried in vain to keep the children away from the windows, but when the North Korean tanks began to roll in, they all walked out to peer at the captivating scene before them. The nuns started chanting in their language, their rosaries clicking between their fingertips as they kept the older boys hidden in the closets, fearful that they would be conscripted by the communists.

There were dead bodies strewn along the pavement, the smell of gunfire and smoke permeated the streets. Bullet holes punctured the cross that the missionaries had placed in front of the building and it was now leaning against the side. The tank stopped. A North Korean army officer descended to greet the people in the streets, he seemed bemused by the cross that lay wasted along the building. With two of his men following close behind, he looked around at all the children who appeared gaunt, hungry, and expectant. One little girl locked eyes with him, for she wanted to see if she could detect anything behind the man's eyes to suggest he had any knowledge of her parents' whereabouts. The officers then shifted their gaze to the foreign missionaries who looked downward as they continued to pray with their rosaries wrapped around their hands.

The Korean social worker who directed the orphanage bowed to them, and there was silence among the children as the army officers conversed with her in hushed tones. Then, the officer looked up at the children once again, "There is nothing to fear. We are here now. You've been liberated by the Korean People's Army. We will bring you food and clothes. You will no longer have to suffer under that traitorous Syngman Rhee."

With that they turned to leave, and Young and the children heard the announcement repeated over and over again on the loudspeaker as the tanks rolled through the streets of Gwangju.

Aside from a sack of rice, the food and clothes never arrived. Young kept her eyes locked on the scenes in the streets, and she soon lost track of who was executing who, and which side was doing the killing. There was killing everywhere, so that only the stench of bodies and blood remained. All these scenes evaporated in her five-year-old mind into a dark and hollow abyss. At the time, Young sought anything to distract her from her hunger. It seemed the shadow of hunger and the void of her parents haunted her morning until night.

Months later, the American GIs arrived. The noise they brought with them was deafening. Their gunfire and smoke shook the streets. But when the noise subsided, the GIs would linger in the streets and come by the orphanage. They had treats in their pockets and the children would crowd all around them. All except for Young, who had been told by her mother to stay away from such men, especially in military uniforms. Young watched them from a distance, holding her knees to her chest, her legs now bony from want of food.

Two marines were flanked by children, and one evoked a particular stir, Marine Corp Staff Sergeant Bradford Davis, an African American man. Many of the children had never seen a black man before and they crowded around him in fascination. His counterpart, Corporeal Jim Brewer, had white hair, white teeth, and the bluest eyes Young had ever seen. Both the men's eyes appeared to be sunken, and Young observed a hint of bewilderment about them despite their sturdy outward appearance. Though it was noticeable only to Young, it made her feel connected to them – this shared feeling of displacement – of want. If the soldiers were aware of their weariness, it did not concern them, they seemed occupied only with the children who crowded around them and whether they had enough to give them. Of course, they did not have enough. There could never be enough. There was never enough to fill the want of a room full of children who longed for their parents.

The young Corporeal spotted Young across the room and walked toward her with a circular tin, "Here, take it. There you go, that's it." Other children had trailed him along the way, holding out their hands, "That's all I've got for now! You've already had yours, remember?" he said, showing his gleaming white teeth.

"This one's for her you guys," he announced to the others, as a way of keeping them away. None of the children understood a word that the soldiers said, and vice versa, but it was a routine of theirs to talk to each other in this manner, the soldiers in English, and the children responding in Korean, having side conversations about the strangers who bestowed onto them the jewels of their c-ration.

Young clutched onto the tin until later that evening when she approached her older brother, "*Oppa*," she whispered. "Look at what I have," she said, revealing the gleam of the silver tin.

Hyun looked up at her behind his glasses, "So open it," he said, as if the action was self-evident.

Young grabbed her older sister Kyu-jin to join them. She opened the tin to reveal a dark brown mysterious square, "*Oppa*, what is it?"

"It's food, eat it," he stated matter-of-factly.

"Do you think it is okay?" Young asked skeptically, "The one with the bright blue eyes gave it to me today."

"Of course it's okay, why haven't you eaten it already?"

"I wanted to share with you and *eonni*."

"No," holding his stomach, "you both share it," he said, shifting his eyes to his books.

"We can't eat it if you don't eat with us, here, just a try little bit," Young suggested, breaking off a piece.

Not having time to react, Hyun took the piece into his mouth, feeling the gooey chocolate and sweet sugar from the fudge coat his tongue, "That's it," he said, "you eat the rest, my stomach..." pointing to his stomach.

Their mother had often fretted about Hyun's sensitive stomach but having not received much in the way of food, it was clear that they were all hungry, and there was nothing in his stomach for which to be sensitive. That he was sacrificing his share for his sisters became a demand at this point, "I mean it, you both eat it, and eat it now before someone comes and takes it away."

Young and Kyu-jin ate every last piece of fudge in the tin, occasionally breaking off a piece for their brother which he promptly refused. The sweetness and the richness of the fudge was shocking at first, but there was a comfort in it, a kind of assurance. And when Young lay awake on her cot at night she licked the roof of her mouth to try and taste the remnants of the sweetness in her mouth.

For that brief moment, as they sat and enjoyed every last crumb of the fudge, Young and her siblings had a reprieve from the world around them. For one moment, they were just children, indulging in a sweet, foreign treat, transporting themselves to the world of Staff Sergeant Bradford Davis and Corporeal Jim Brewer, where indulgences such as fudge are born. That the two men would hold such hope for Young was something tangible that five-year-old Young could lean on, something to distract her from her hunger and from the pain of missing her parents. She no longer stayed in the corner when the GIs visited but neither did she reach out her hands like the other children. Young learned that if she stayed in the back of the crowd, looking on quietly, that they would find her, and she would be rewarded for her patience.

They would find her, and she would be rewarded for her patience. Young would tell herself this in the ensuing months. But this was still the very beginning of the war, and Seoul would change hands four more times before the war would end in a stalemate.

And Young would be unable to recall any of it.

Beloved Young, her parents' fiercest guardian. Young, youngest to Sa Mi and Sun. Beloved *mangnae*, born in the year of the fire dog. In the throes of civil war. All alone among the fire and smoke, longing for her parents.

EPILOGUE

Sa Mi's *Mangnae*

Indianapolis, IN

Summer 1970

I t hadn't always been this way. Between them. The shouting hadn't actually started until long after they had immigrated to America, and when it happened, it caught Jae completely off-guard. He had learned early on that his young, beautiful bride was ridden with thorns and the irritation and unrest she experienced as a result of her family's history was not something she tried to hide from him. But in Korea she directed her heartache at her parents and siblings and was too embarrassed to even look her husband in the face. When they came to America to start anew, Jae assumed that all the baggage would be left behind.

However, when all the grit and loneliness set-in which seemed to have no beginning and no end like the Midwestern horizon, Jae blamed himself for his wife's unhappiness. That the seed of bitterness had been planted before her encounter with the stoic pharmacist did not matter. It was Jae after all who had put in his papers to come to America, long before meeting Young. He was the one that nursed a burning curiosity and desire to see and experience the rest of the world. Young was too consumed by the weight of the past, the size of her family's despair, and the corrosive provincialism that made her see only the dogged and narrow dictates of tradition and not the expansive possibilities of the future. Coming to America was not the dream adventure that it was for Jae, a way to pay homage to the American GIs of his childhood, who stood out like a wall of heroes in his mind. For Young, it was just another way of saying "fuck you" to the dysfunctional entanglement of her family. It was not unlike the time she had swallowed a bottle of pills shortly after her wedding to get the attention of her mother, who, despite Young's repeated pleas to use the monthly allowance she provided for her mother's own expenses, passed it on to Young's siblings to indulge one destructive vice or other. That Young chose to share incidents like these with Audrey during her age of becoming was just another way to remind her daughter that the past was always right there, bubbling over at the surface, threatening to drown them all.

There were other incidents that Young didn't share with her daughter. It was the dramatic ones that always seemed to make the cut. To Young, her days in America came and vanished like a dream, and unlike Jae whose memories were lucid, Young never seemed to be able to recall the slower days that strung together the first few years of their lives in America. The solitude of those days evaporated beyond the gauzy cirrus clouds that brushed the summer Midwestern sky.

The heat of the summers had a particular angle to it, not unlike the extreme weather patterns in Korea. But unlike the geography of Korea whose jagged mountains sought defiantly to reach out toward the heavens above, the flat plains were vulnerable next to that infinite sky, and the humility of the land was palpable even to the people who occupied it. Young was never one for the sweltering heat of summer and the blinding sun. The summers of those early years in America recalled the stench of trash and grease stagnating in the air. Those were the smells that greeted her when she pushed open the heavy metal door leading out to the back entrance of "Chung King Chinese Restaurant," where empty cans of mushrooms and bamboo shoots filled the dumpster on the other side of the alley.

The lunch rush ended early. Young already completed all of her side work and helped the others finish theirs as well. There was nothing else left to do. Despite the idle chatter among the waitresses, Young felt her isolation closing in on her. It was precisely for this reason – to escape her own loneliness – that she sought out the job in the first place and she was exceedingly grateful to Mr. Choo for offering it to her. And yet, like many of the days that followed after arriving in America, Young fought from asphyxiating from the quiet desperation of it all.

Jae was always fifteen minutes early. He never left Young waiting. Even when she insisted he come at 3:00pm to pick her up from her shift, the yellow VW bug was always put-puttering in the lot with Jae behind the wheel, eagerly awaiting her arrival by 2:45pm.

"If he is anything, he is predictable," Young had said to her mother soon after their wedding.

"Reliable," her mother had come back with. "He is reliable. A good man is reliable."

Taking her mother's tone as a slight to her father Young sighed. At nineteen and the youngest in her family, she had already cultivated her sharp brow, but was still a young girl in the ways of the world, especially when it came to men. The only man she deemed worthwhile was her own father, despite all of his shortcomings. This was the nature of Young's loyalty. She clung to the binds of family as the only and end truth among life's chaos and indifference. Nobody protested life's injustices with more vitriol and passion than Young, and yet, nobody remained more faithful to the means by which the cycle of cruelty continued. Later on, Young's daughter would define herself against the very pessimism that her mother espoused.

Still, in that moment under the heat of the July sun circa 1971, it was neither the familiar pessimism nor the comfort of bitterness that consumed Young. Out there in the wide Midwestern sky Young was seized by her own vulnerabilities, and a nagging helplessness that left her lost.

Only in America would she be singing the praises of the toothless Mr. Choo, who, though he was ethnic Chinese often tried out his choppy Korean on her. He reminded her on several occasions of how he had lived in Pusan for several years as a young man where he had owned his very own fishing boat. If she had passed him on the street in Korea she would never have even noticed him, in fact, she would have looked the other way. But as the person who signs her paycheck every two weeks Young bows her head to him and even offers a faint smile of encouragement when he says, "Ah Mrs. Son, *ahn-nyung-ha-seyo!*"

Only in America would Young befriend a certain Eunja McCallister, wife of an American GI. War bride. As a wife of a professional man, in Korea Young would never have condescended to socialize with one of the women "from the bases," but here in America, she finds herself sharing stories and laughter with a woman she would otherwise have nothing in common. Here in America they share the same hopes, work side-by-side, and take down orders for hungry white Midwesterns. In fact, in America Eunja has the leg-up, with her superior English and her understanding of all the nuances and slang that strikes Young as vulgar and unrefined. In America, Young's understandings of the neat social stratifications and traditions are being challenged. The very things that in their rigidity had provided a comfort and a certainty to Young in the past make little difference in America. This makes Young all the lonelier. One makes compromises when one is lonely. America is a place where one swallows one's pride, as Young has discovered time and again.

As she averts her eyes to avoid the glaring sun, Young pulls the pale blue air mail envelope out of her apron pocket and looks at her mother's handwriting. She imagines her now elderly mother painstakingly copying the letters of her address in Indianapolis onto the envelope with a cigarette burning in one hand and her pen in the other. She would have been seated on the floor, with her small table before her – the same one she always used when she composed her letters. Young had always admired her mother's delicate, tiny hands. The tumult of the years that marked the generation between them was enacted in the differences among their hands. Young's hands were aged beyond her years, while her mother's elegant hands were flawless.

The writing on the envelope is distinct. It is not the script of a native speaker, but foreign strokes adapted to the complex curves of English. The writing is nonetheless impressive for someone whose claim to the English language is "Kennedy" and "Good Mohning!"

Young looked up toward the searing July heat and noticed the greasy parking lot of broken boxes and scavenging pigeons. She longed so desperately for her mother in that moment. The distance between them seemed interminable, deafening.

There was a fragility about this letter. Young sensed it from the handwriting. It must have been a difficult week for her mother because it did not begin with a musing on the week's drama, or her mother's characteristic irony, or any neighborhood gossip. It was not her mother's nature to observe the social convention of masking her family's trials and imperfections and she spoke freely of them to neighbors and friends. To Sa Mi, it was common wisdom that the Truth was not always pretty and she felt that hiding it never gave it the dignity it deserved. To be so forthright was a kind of therapy for her, but the letter in Young's hands had a somber tone to it, with none of the color that normally found its way into Sa Mi's writing.

Young pictured her mother in a painfully anxious state, nervously taking drags from her cigarette or tearfully lamenting the cruelty of her husband who she was forced to wed at fifteen. Young imagined her mother pacing in the tiny confines of their home until her father would erupt on her mother in irritation. Young's father had little patience for his wife's indulgence of such episodes for fear of the anxiety gripping him. Sun felt it a form of weakness to allow one's fears to seep outside of one's own control, and as of late, he sought to channel his own desperations through sips of plum wine and the practice of calligraphy.

As Young imagined her mother in this restless state, waiting in vain for her daughter to rescue her from the asphyxiation of boredom and living itself, she reflected upon the first few lines of her mother's letter. How unusual they were. Normally, her mother started a letter mid-thought, in a stream-of-consciousness fashion, as an ongoing conversation colored by an urgency to get the thought on paper before it disappears, as in, "Dear beloved *mangnae*: When Myung's mother confided to me that her son-in-law was parading her daughter with insults on a daily basis, it took everything for me not to tell her to keep her worries to herself. Everyone knows who that poor girl really loves!"

This letter however, was different, full of pauses and reflections. It started: "To my beloved *mangnae*: I have a box filled with letters from you since you moved away from me to that giant America. I have been going through them all morning. You have excellent handwriting. It must be hard for you to get through any letters of mine. Did you know that your mother, at some point long, long ago, was a studious little girl? I used to be first in my class. Now my mind is stuffed with empty spaces wedged between bundles and bundles of memories."

It was not in her mother's nature to reflect upon the past, nor was it in Young's nature to delve into what was sure to be a vat of disappointment and sorrow. She was surprised to hear about her mother's childhood, having never pictured her mother as a little girl. Young was no less self-involved than anyone else to imagine her mother outside the confines of her own existence, as if finding our loved ones outside the boundaries we create might obscure them to us, make us lose sight of them.

In reading the words from her mother, Young was ashamed that she had never before considered her mother's story on its own, separate and apart from her involvement.

This fact, together with her mother's unease which seeped off the page, sequestered Young to her current state of solitude. She never felt more alone than she did in this country, with its wide streets and endless horizons. She had heard that America was vast but imagined that Indiana was not much different than the rest of it. "People leave you alone here," she had once written to her mother, "It is not like it is there, where everyone is hovering over your every move." To try and provide a balanced view, in the same letter: "We tried to order a hamburger the other day and the lady behind the counter kept asking us questions that we could not understand so we just kept nodding our heads – yes, yes, yes – who knew that ordering lunch could be so complicated!"

Young pulls out a handkerchief and her Rado watch. She and her husband had bought matching pairs for their wedding and only hers survived. She recalled the pained look on his face (he was not demonstrative by any stretch of the imagination) when he told her that someone had ripped it off his wrist on a crowded bus in Seoul. "Such things do not happen in America," she had written to her mother, "everyone drives cars here. Americans are an innocent people, not jaded and desperate like they are back home."

2:42. Young carefully wipes her eyes and blows her nose. She cannot let Jae see her in this state nor can she share all that has transpired in her heart and mind. Unlike her mother, Young keeps her vulnerabilities buried behind steely eyes and an impenetrable will. She has never known anything else.

Young had insisted on the job. That she served greasy Chinese food to indifferent white Americans was really a blessing. Those days when she was in their tiny apartment while her husband worked as an assistant in a local pharmacy or was in class at the university, she thought she might go crazy of boredom. Still, her labor at the restaurant stood between her and her husband like a silent pillar. She would never tell him that her loneliness persisted, even in the company of Mr. Choo's rotted tooth smile, the somnambulant wait staff, and the aloof customers. And he couldn't tell her to quit, knowing that the alternative of staying caged in their apartment left her no choice but to be plagued by homesickness.

Instead, she chose to mask the heavy stone within her heart. She told him how relieved she was to be working there at Chungking and even shared stories of the quirks of customers and the profiles of her fellow co-workers.

Like clockwork, Young hears the clanking of the bright yellow VW bug that her husband purchased for $100 and it soon comes into full view.

She immediately notices the concerned look on his face when he sees her waiting. He is always there first, even before she pushes the back door open.

"It was slow. I got out a few minutes earlier today," Young greets Jae's unsaid inquiry.

Jae nods his head, and ever so gently, pats her knee.

Young looks toward the endless horizon and imagines her mother as a little girl, buried in her studies. It is a stark contrast to the streams of disappearing smoke and the weight of pen pushing onto paper. Tonight she will make *meeyukgook* from the seaweed Lin brought her last week from a recent trip to China. It has a different taste from the seaweed she is used to, but there are no Korean markets nearby and the soup is her husband's favorite.

Her husband jokingly refers to it as their "Chinese *meeyukgook*." She will write about it to her mother. Young will also have to insist that her mother not send her the Korean seaweed, for fear of her wasting her money on the postage.

This is the only way they can limit their moments of restlessness, by writing back and forth about nothing. It is easier that way.

In the meantime, and over time, the loneliness erupts. And the children will learn that marriage breeds bitterness. They will never know that there once was a time when Jae rested his hand on Young's knee. They will never know that there once was a quiet mutual respect between their parents that could keep the past at bay. They will never find out that there was a time when Young cared more about satiating her husband's palate than that of strangers. The children will never learn that it hadn't always been this way between their parents. That once, long ago, there was love.

###

A World Without Lupus

This book was written over several years and in negotiation with lupus, a chronic autoimmune disease that largely affects women of childbearing age of African American, Asian, Hispanic, and Native American descent.

A portion of the proceeds from the sale of this book will go to the Lupus Research Alliance to improve diagnosis and treatment, and to allow researchers to seek a cure.

Thank you for reading and for your support.

With love and gratitude,

JMH

94584799R00132

Made in the USA
Lexington, KY
31 July 2018